THE BIG WIN

ROB CHILDS
THE BIG WIN

Illustrated by Aidan Potts

YOUNG CORGI BOOKS

For all young footballers —
boys and *girls*

ROB CHILDS
THE BIG
FOOTBALL FRENZY

Including

THE BIG WIN

THE BIG FIX

THE BIG FREEZE

YOUNG CORGI BOOKS

THE BIG FOOTBALL FRENZY
A YOUNG CORGI BOOK : 0 552 54702 6

PRINTING HISTORY
Young Corgi edition published 2000

3 5 7 9 10 8 6 4

Copyright © Rob Childs, 2000

including

THE BIG WIN
First published in Great Britain by Young Corgi Books, 1998
Copyright © Rob Childs, 1998
Illustrations copyright © Aidan Potts, 1998

THE BIG FIX
First published in Great Britain by Young Corgi Books, 1998
Copyright © Rob Childs, 1998
Illustrations copyright © Aidan Potts, 1998

THE BIG FREEZE
First published in Great Britain by Young Corgi Books, 1997
Copyright © Rob Childs, 1997
Illustrations copyright © Aidan Potts, 1997

The right of Rob Childs to be identified as the author of these works has been
asserted in accordance with the Copyright, Designs and Patents Act 1988

With thanks to the staff and pupils at Northold High School for their help in
the preparation of the cover; photographs taken by Oliver Hunter on
location at Northolt High School

Young Corgi Books are published by Random House Children's Books,
61–63 Uxbridge Road, London W5 5SA,
a division of The Random House Group Ltd,
in Australia by Random House Australia (Pty) Ltd,
20 Alfred Street, Milsons Point, Sydney, NSW 2061, Australia,
and in New Zealand by Random House New Zealand Ltd,
18 Poland Road, Glenfield, Auckland 10, New Zealand
and in South Africa by Random House (Pty) Ltd,
Endulini, 5a Jubilee Road, Parktown 2193, South Africa.

Printed and bound in Great Britain by
Cox & Wyman Ltd, Reading, Berkshire.

www.**kidsatrandomhouse**.co.uk

1 Winter Games

'Come on – run! Too cold to stand about. Find those spaces.'

The headmaster of Danebridge Primary School normally looked forward to taking the Year 5 Games lesson. Even on a bitter Monday afternoon in mid-January. But Mr Jones had something else on his mind today. He'd rather have been sitting behind his office desk next to the warm radiator.

'Huh! All right for old Jonesy,'

grunted Philip. 'Just look at him, all wrapped up in his thick coat and scarf.'

Chris grinned. 'Not to mention a weird, red bobble hat! Never seen him in that thing before.'

'Perhaps it was a Christmas present. Y'know, one of them yukky things from some aunt, like a jumper that's miles too big.'

They giggled. 'It'd have to be massive not to fit you,' said his pal.

Chris Weston was certainly pleased with his own presents. The school team captain was wearing his new soccer boots and his snazzy, green goalie gloves. He couldn't wait to give them their debut in tomorrow's league match, Danebridge's first game of the New Year.

'Get going, you two. No time to stop for a chat.'

Mr Jones had spotted them. Even with over thirty pupils dodging about inside the square training grids, anybody standing still shone out like a lighthouse. Especially someone Philip's height!

They darted once more into the crowd of hurtling bodies, swerving this way and that to try and avoid contact. The gangly centre-back, with his long thin legs, found it an almost impossible task. His accidental trip on a daydreaming passer-by was worthy of a yellow card!

'Soz, Kerry,' he apologized quickly. 'Are you OK?'

The girl scrambled to her feet. 'Yes – no thanks to you,' she snapped, angry at the dirty smear down the side of her new tracksuit. 'Just see what you've made me do. You're like a clumsy, baby giraffe.'

'Said I'm sorry, didn't I? You should've been looking where you were going.'

Before their argument could heat up further, Mr Jones blew his whistle and ordered the players into groups of four. 'Mixed,' he stressed. 'Don't spend long choosing, I'm not asking you to marry each other!'

Chris and Philip were joined reluctantly by Kerry and a friend as Mr

Jones continued to bark out instructions. 'Four-a-side games in the grids now – and no goalies. I want you all on the move.'

For once, Danebridge's keeper didn't mind about the ban on goalies. He'd injured a hand during the holidays at an indoor soccer tournament and he wasn't going to risk hurting his fingers again before the match.

Chris turned to Kerry. 'Me and Phil can be the defence while you two stay up in attack. How about that?'

'Suits me,' said Kerry with a shrug. 'I like scoring goals.'

'I know. I keep saying you should come and play for the school team.'

She shook her head. 'I go riding Saturday mornings.'

'Not all our games are on Saturdays. Like tomorrow, for instance.'

'Yeah, two-thirty kick-off, away,' Philip grinned. 'We're missing most of afternoon school.'

'Still not for me,' she said. 'I'll stick to horses and netball.'

'Pity!' Chris sighed. 'We need a good goalscorer.'

That was true. Danebridge had picked up after a poor start to the season, but they were still finding goals hard to come by. Rakesh Patel in Year 6 was their leading scorer, but he'd only found the net four times.

Kerry immediately showed her eye for goal. Less than a minute into the game, she gave her marker the slip and stroked the ball clean through the centre of the narrow, coned target.

Chris whistled under his breath. 'Magic! I've got to change her mind about playing for us somehow. She's deadly!'

6

Kerry proved too much of a handful for anybody to keep under control on such a small pitch. Her speed off the mark allowed her to reach a pass with time and space to shoot before a defender could make a challenge. Their opponents even stopped trying after she notched up a hat-trick.

'Great stuff, Kerry!' Philip applauded her. 'If I'm a baby giraffe, you're making this lot look like wooden donkeys!'

The teams soon swapped round, forming different foursomes for another game. Chris now discovered for himself just how difficult it could be to play against her. Kerry seemed to delight in showing up the limitations of the school captain when he had the ball at his feet and not in his hands. It was an uncomfortable experience.

His most embarrassing moment came when he delayed too long on the ball before passing it. Kerry whipped it off his toes, but he recovered enough to block her route to goal and make her nearly run the ball out of play. Chris thought he had Kerry trapped on the touchline, but it was wishful thinking. She cheekily knocked the ball through his legs, nipped round him to regain possession and then coolly sidefooted it in.

Chris greeted the headmaster's shrill whistle with some relief. Mr Jones had decided to cut the session short and ushered everyone back inside to thaw out. Nobody complained, not even the keenest of footballers.

'Brrr! Hope it's not so cold tomorrow,' said Chris, crouched against the radiator in the boys' cloakroom. 'I'll freeze to death in goal.'

'Depends how busy you are,' smiled Philip. 'Langby School are near the top of the league, so I doubt if you'll have a chance to get frostbite!'

As the bell rang for home-time, Rakesh burst into the cloakroom.

'Hey!' he yelled out in excitement. 'You guys heard the big news about Mark Towers?'

'Only that he's away today,' muttered Chris, regretting that Mark might have to miss the match. 'What's so big about that? We can manage without him.'

'Our teacher's just told us why he's away,' Rakesh grinned, barely able to contain himself. 'His family have gone and won the National Lottery!'

2 It Could Be You!

Chris lay in bed that night, unable to sleep. The street light cast flickering shadows into the room he shared with Andrew, his elder brother, who'd left the primary school the year before. They were both thinking about the same thing.

'You still awake?' he hissed across the room.

'No,' Andrew yawned.

'What would *you* do if you'd won all that money?'

'Spend it.'

'What on?'

'Football gear. For a start, I'd buy all United's latest strips, plus expensive boots and trainers. Dead flash, like – only the best. Could wear a different pair every day if I wanted to.'

'C'mon, be serious. You can't blow it all on boots and kit.'

'Well, I'd also need a season ticket to sit in one of United's plush executive boxes. Might even buy them a new player. Mind you, can't get anybody decent for only a million or so these days.'

'There *are* other things in life besides football, you know.'

'Not much at our age,' Andrew grumbled. 'No point buying a car — can't drive. Too young to go off round the world. Mum wouldn't let me.'

'OK, OK, if you're just going to be silly. Might as well try to get to sleep. G'night.'

Andrew was quiet for a while, then said, 'Tell you something, our kid.'

'What?'

'Don't reckon I'd like to be a millionaire after all.'

'Why not?'

'Well, as Grandad said earlier to

me, you wouldn't know who your real friends are.'

'How d'yer mean?'

'You'd always be wondering which they liked best – you or your money! G'night, little brother.'

'This is going to be one of those days,' sighed Mr Jones as he drove into Danebridge the following morning. 'I can feel it in my bones.'

He was right. Tuesday began badly and steadily got worse. He even had to abandon school assembly because the children were so noisy and excited. A strange kind of fever seemed to have come over them, but its symptoms were all too obvious – wide eyes, shaking heads and green faces.

The headmaster hadn't needed to consult a medical dictionary, however, for the cause of the bug. Its name was jealousy.

Mark had turned up at school unexpectedly and was clearly revelling in his new-found fame. He'd already been heard on local radio the previous evening after rumours of the family's good fortune in the weekend Lottery draw had spread beyond the village.

'How does it feel to be so rich at your age, Mark?' he was asked during the interview.

'Real cool.'

'Is it true that you chose the lucky numbers?'

'Yes, but they're special, not lucky,' he corrected the reporter, pleased to have the chance to show off his mathe-

matical knowledge. 'We always have them. They're the first six square numbers – 4, 9, 16, 25, 36 and 49. That's not counting number one, of course.'

'Of course,' the woman repeated, not wishing to admit that she had no idea what the boy was talking about. She'd quickly moved on to ask his parents whether they were going to give up working.

Mr Jones was worried that the same question might also apply to his pupils. Very little work was being done at school due to the effects of this Lottery fever, especially in Mark's class. The children simply weren't able to concentrate.

Mark found himself surrounded in the playground at morning break by a large group of grinning admirers. They all knew who he was, even if he couldn't put a name to most of them.

Close by his side, though, was Paul Walker, a fellow member of the school football team. Paul appeared quite happy to confess his ignorance about square numbers.

'Don't tell me *you* don't know what they are either,' Mark scoffed. 'We did them again in class last term.'

'I'm no good at maths,' Paul laughed. 'Not like you, Professor.'

It wasn't only Mark's brilliance at maths which had earned him that particular nickname. He was hopelessly absent-minded. Even on the soccer pitch he was liable to wander out of position as his attention drifted away from the game onto something else.

'They're called square numbers 'cos you can make square patterns out of

them,' Mark explained proudly to the whole group. 'Like four is two rows of two, and nine is made up of three rows of three – and so on.'

'If these numbers are so famous,' piped up a younger boy, 'lots of other people must have picked them too.'

'Not as many as you'd think. There were just five winning tickets.'

And then came the question that everybody kept asking. 'How much have you actually won?'

'Over two million pounds!' Mark boasted, enjoying the sound of all that money tripping off his tongue. 'Or to be precise – two million, three hundred and twenty thousand, four hundred and twelve pounds! That's only by my calculations, like, but I know I'm right.'

'Just listen to him,' groaned Philip as he and Chris passed by. 'He's

lapping up all this star treatment. Last week, everybody would have said the Professor was dead boring.'

'Yeah, but now he's dead boring with loadsamoney!' Chris said, recalling Andrew's remark. 'That's the difference.'

As always, Chris's grandad helped out with transport to the game that afternoon. He turned round to speak to his young passengers before they set off.

'If anyone mentions the Lottery on this journey, I'll make them get out and walk the rest of the way,' he promised with a wink.

'Just as well that Mark's in Jonesy's car, then,' Chris grinned.

'Aye, it is. I can't go anywhere

without hearing people going on about you-know-what. It's driving me mad.'

'Imagine what it's like for me, being in his class,' muttered Rakesh.

Chris shook his head in mock sympathy. 'You'll have to stick some cotton wool in your ears to shut him out.'

'Pardon?' his friend said, pretending to remove a piece, and then laughed. 'I don't think the Professor even knows what day it is. He's on another planet. He's got too many numbers flying around inside his head.'

'They must have plenty of space,' Philip put in. 'It's suddenly grown twice as big!'

'He'd forgotten all about this match, you know,' Rakesh told them. 'Jonesy's had to find a spare kit and kids were almost queuing up to lend him their boots.'

'Hardly surprising after what's happened. He never remembers to bring his own, anyway.'

Rakesh nodded. 'Yeah, but he usually has to go round *begging* people for a pair.'

'The Professor reckons his parents'

memories are even worse than his,' Philip chuckled, shaking his head in amazement. 'Trust a family like that to have all the luck!'

'We might be better off without him, the way he is at the moment,' said Chris. 'I mean, on form, he does a good job in midfield with his strong tackles and that. But it'll probably be like playing with ten men today.'

Grandad interrupted. 'I hope not. It's going to need a really good team performance to get a result against Langby. You've all got to do your bit.'

The headmaster felt the same way. But as he led the small convoy of cars towards the market town of Langby, Mr Jones doubted whether the boys were in the right frame of mind to play such an important football

match. With the temperatures still barely above freezing, he feared that Langby might catch them cold in more ways than one.

Another defeat could prove costly. Danebridge were still too close for comfort to the league's relegation zone . . .

3 Team Spirit

Chris found himself under bombardment straightaway.

When the ball was rolled to one side at the kick-off, a Langby player suddenly whacked it goalwards from well inside the centre-circle. He hoped to catch the Danebridge keeper off guard and off his line.

His plan almost worked too. As Chris desperately back-pedalled, the ball dropped from the sky out of his reach, bounced up high and sailed

less than a metre wide of the target. Chris heaved a huge sigh of relief.

'That's just a sighter,' laughed the home team captain. 'Welcome to Langby. We're the league's top scorers.'

Chris soon saw why. He faced a barrage of shots from all angles and distances and did well to keep Langby at bay for as long as ten minutes. His new gloves were now splattered with dirt, and a point-blank range blaster made his damaged fingers tingle as he touched it over the bar.

It was from the corner that Langby deservedly went in front. Philip's head cleared the first cross, but only as far as the edge of the penalty area. Mark was daydreaming. He failed to pick up the attacker lurking there and made no attempt to block the shot. The ball was driven firmly through a ruck of bodies past the helpless Chris and into his net.

Mark looked down at his borrowed boots in dismay for a moment. But when he raised his head, the Danebridge players saw there was a silly grin spreading across his face.

'Oh, well, not to worry,' he said with a shrug. 'It's only a game. Who cares about losing when you're a millionaire?'

'Come on, Mark Towers, get stuck in!' cried Mr Jones from the touchline as Danebridge restarted the game.

'They're just walking through us.'

It was obvious to everyone that Mark wasn't pulling his weight for the team. Out on the pitch, however, many of the players were letting him know rather more forcibly that they weren't exactly thrilled by his efforts.

'You're about as much use as a chocolate tea-pot!'

'You are allowed to move, you know. You're not nailed to the spot.'

Rakesh nudged into Mark as he jogged by, almost knocking him over.

'Out of the way. You're cluttering the place up, just standing there.'

'You did that on purpose,' Mark protested, glaring at Rakesh.

The winger feigned innocence. 'Why would I do a thing like that?'

'I could give you two million reasons.'

'Don't let them rile you, Mark,' said Paul, running up to him in support. 'They're just jealous, that's all.'

'They can say what they like,' he smirked. 'Doesn't bother me now.'

Chris couldn't get close enough to give Mark an earful, but Philip did his job for him. 'We'll have you off at half-time, Professor, if you don't start getting a few tackles in,' he warned.

Mark scowled. 'Right, you're another one who won't be having a sniff of any money when I dish some of it out to my friends.'

'I don't want your money,' Philip sneered. 'I just want you to try and help us win this game.'

That was looking more and more of an unlikely prospect. Langby kept streaming forward, sweeping through the gaps in midfield that Mark should have been filling.

Langby were so much on top that it came as no surprise when they scored a second goal. It was an excellent solo strike by their skilful winger, whose burst of speed left Paul for dead. He

dummied his way past Philip, too, before unleashing a fierce shot beyond Chris's dive.

'I suppose you think that was Mark's fault as well, do you?' said Paul.

Philip bristled at the full-back's sarcasm. 'You're a creep, the way you keep sticking up for him all the time. I wonder why?'

'What d'yer mean by that?'

'Huh! Do I have to spell it out for you? Everybody knows why you're suddenly crawling round the Professor.'

Paul didn't take kindly to that remark either and it was a good thing that the captain managed to step between them in time.

'Cut it out, both of you, and get on with the game,' Chris said firmly.

'We've got no chance if we're falling out with each other. We're two-nil down already.'

Soon it was three. And this third goal was a real sickener for any hopes of staging a comeback. Mark finally stirred himself enough to join in the action and attempted to guide the ball back to Paul. His pass was weak and misdirected, giving the Langby captain a late Christmas present.

'Ta very much,' the boy cackled gratefully. But only after he'd tucked the ball away into the net.

Mr Jones was not amused. 'I could see this kind of sloppy display coming,' he fumed at half-time. 'You're just not with it, some of you.'

Mark gave a defiant shrug as the headmaster glanced his way. Nor did he endear himself to Mr Jones when his muttered comment was just a little too loud to ignore. 'I didn't want to come to school today in the first place. Don't see why I should have to any more.'

Mr Jones struggled to control his temper, but he knew this wasn't the right time or place to discipline the boy. For now, Mark was one of the three players substituted as he tried to reorganize his dispirited side. Paul and Philip were the others. The headmaster had noted their argument and decided they could cool off by shivering together on the touchline. He'd deal with them – and Mark – later.

To their credit, Danebridge did make more of a fight of it in the second half. Without Mark's unsettling influence, they played far better as a team and managed to restrict Langby's goal-scoring chances. They even created some of their own too.

Rakesh went close with a shot that grazed the post and then he set substitute Ryan up for a goal on his debut. All Ryan had to do was tap the ball home after Rakesh's clever dribble down the wing pulled two defenders and the goalkeeper out of position. The young scorer's smile of pure delight briefly lit up a bleak afternoon for the visitors.

Sadly, things took a turn for the worse right at the end of the game with an injury to Chris. Langby broke clear in search of a fourth goal to clinch their victory and Chris dived bravely at the striker's feet to smother his shot. The ball ran loose for someone else to poke into the empty net and Chris was left on the ground, nursing his trampled fingers.

As the opposing captains shook hands at the final whistle, Chris was trying to hide the pain, both of the 4–1 defeat and also in his fingers. He was only glad he didn't have to shake with his left hand.

'Back home for some more first-aid,' Grandad said as Chris trudged off the field. 'Cup match on Saturday, remember, and we've got to have you fit to play in that.'

Chris grimaced. He hated the

thought of missing the cup-tie, but that wasn't the only problem on his mind. He'd just overheard Mark openly offering tempting bribes to several players to be friends with him again.

4 Who's in Goal?

Mark was absent from school the next day. Nor did his parents go into work. Neighbours reported that the family car stayed in the garage and callers found the curtains drawn and the doorbell unanswered. Even the phone was left off the hook.

If the strange disappearance of the Towers family was a mystery to people in the village, Danebridge's young footballers had more important matters to discuss. Still licking their wounds from the league defeat, they were wondering how they could avoid the same fate in the cup.

Chris's injury added to the worries. The captain was ever-present in goal and nobody else much fancied the job.

'Who's going to play there if you can't?' asked Philip.

'It could be you!' Chris grinned, shuffling forward in the lunch queue.

'I hope that was meant as a joke. C'mon, any ideas?'

Chris had already been giving the choice some serious thought and he was still none the wiser. 'Dunno really. Might have said Mark before, but I guess that's out of the question now. I don't suppose he'll be wanting to play for the school again. That's if he ever does come back here!'

'Don't reckon Jonesy would have him in the team anyway.'

Chris shrugged. 'Rakesh, maybe? He's OK.'

'Yeah, but we need him up front to knock one or two in for us.'

'That's been our main problem all season,' Chris sighed. 'Not being able to score more goals than the other team do!'

As if summoned by magic, Rakesh suddenly popped up to join them, jumping the queue. 'How's the hand?' he asked, ignoring complaints.

'Not too good. Hurts a bit when I hold anything.'

'Pity it's not your writing hand.'

Chris smiled. 'I'm still hoping it'll be OK for Saturday.'

'You could always play centre-forward,' Rakesh suggested, only half in jest. 'Might make a nice change, trying to put the ball into the net instead of keeping it out!'

'No, I'm rubbish on the pitch,' laughed Chris. 'At least that's what Andrew says.'

'Well, he would. At least it'd be better than biting your nails on the touchline, just watching.'

Chris held out his plate for ladled helpings of food from the hatches, taking extra care not to drop it. He added an apple and a drink to his tray

and then looked around for some-
where to sit. He spotted just the place.
Right next to Kerry, the very person
he wanted to talk to!

The following lunchtime was the
soccer squad's regular Thursday
training session while it remained too
dark after school.

Mr Jones was keen to use it to give
any volunteer goalkeepers some much
needed practice – just in case. 'I won't
name the team for the cup-tie until we
see how Chris's hand feels tomorrow,'
he explained, and then gave a grin.
'And I also want to check out our new
signing here!'

All eyes turned towards the player
in the red tracksuit.

'She can play in goal for us!' Rakesh
piped up.

Kerry joined in the giggling. 'I'm

fine catching the ball in netball, but I don't think I'm ready to take Chris's place yet.'

'Why not? We could do a swap,' Rakesh smirked. 'Chris has always fancied playing netball!'

Jokes over, Kerry was soon impressing everyone with her shooting skills. Although Mr Jones was already well aware of the girl's ability, this was the first time an interested spectator had seen her in action.

Grandad was leaning on the fence that divided the playing field from a public footpath. He was the school's number one supporter. He rarely missed a match, home or away, and even liked to watch the footballers practise whenever he could.

Normally that was easy. He just had to wander down to the bottom of his garden to see them play on the village recreation ground behind his cottage. Their own playing field wasn't big enough for a full-size pitch. This lunchtime, however, he'd made the effort to come up to the school after Chris had told him about their new recruit.

'Aye, she's a good 'un, all right, no doubt about that,' he murmured to himself as Kerry cracked another shot into one of the small five-a-side goals. She can hit 'em with either foot.'

Several players had turns in the two goals, with the rest in groups waiting for a chance to shoot at them. To Grandad's experienced eye, none of the keepers on view could be chosen for the match with any confidence.

Chris came over to him during a short break in the practice. 'What do you reckon, then, Grandad?'

'About the goalies or the girl?'

'Both.'

'Well, m'boy,' he wheezed, blowing out his cheeks. 'I'd say that if you're not between the sticks, then Danebridge are in big trouble.'

Chris had expected Grandad to come out with something like that, but he still pulled a face. 'And Kerry? I'm surprised she actually agreed to play as it clashes with her horseriding. But she's worth the risk, eh?'

'What risk is that?'

'I deliberately got her mad at lunch yesterday,' he grinned. 'Said it was much harder to score a goal in a real match than just a kickabout in Games – and I bet her that she couldn't do it. Now she's out to prove me wrong.'

'So what happens if she does?'

His grin faded. 'I have to get up on top of a horse and jump a fence!'

Grandad nudged Chris on the arm to make him look round. Kerry was juggling a ball on her feet and knees, keeping it up in the air, just as Rakesh called out a playful challenge from the goal.

'C'mon, then, Kerry. Try and beat me. Bet you can't.'

She flicked the ball up a little

higher and as it dropped, struck it crisply on the half-volley. Rakesh dived in vain. He never even got close to the ball as it flashed past him into the corner of the net.

'It obviously doesn't pay to bet against this girl,' Grandad chuckled. 'Looks like you'll need to book some riding lessons, m'boy!'

5 Humble Pie

Mark arrived back at school on Friday morning, but village gossip reached the playground before him. The Towers hadn't won the Lottery after all. Their numbers had come up last week, but they'd forgotten to buy a ticket! It was said they only realized when they tried to claim their prize.

The Professor was greeted by jeers and taunts.

'Hey! Look who's here – it's the ex-millionaire!'

'You've got to be in to win!'

Mark glared at his tormentors. But his parents had warned him that he must not retaliate, no matter how bad any provocation might be. He sat alone in the headmaster's office while the junior classes were in assembly.

'Mark's going to need our help to get over all this business and put it behind him,' Mr Jones told his pupils. 'I know it's difficult, but try and forget that it ever happened. Just treat him like you used to before.'

As he returned to the office, Mr Jones felt like crossing his fingers. He could only hope that the children would respond in the right way. 'It was very brave of you to come to school today, Mark,' he said sympathetically. 'Not many would have done in your position.'

'Had to show up sometime,' sighed Mark. 'Mum and Dad left it to me.'

'Well, I think you may discover who your true friends are now at any rate,' Mr Jones said. 'Money can have a strange effect on people, you know. They can change – and not always for the better.'

Mark gulped, taking the point. 'Sorry about last Tuesday, Mr Jones. I hope you'll let me play again. That's why I'm here really.'

The headmaster nodded. 'I'm willing to forgive and forget, Mark, but it's your teammates that you need to apologize to as well.'

Mark was invited to the team meeting at breaktime and stood sheepishly in front of all the players. It was quite a shock for him to see Kerry sitting among them.

'I know I don't deserve another chance, the way I acted so stupid,' he began. 'I'm sorry. Just hope I'll be able to try and make up for it.'

Chris glanced round to check that others felt the same as he did. They were smiling. 'Nice to have the old Mark back,' the captain said. 'You could make a start tomorrow perhaps. How do you fancy playing in goal?'

Mark's jaw dropped. 'In . . . in goal! B . . . but . . .'

'No buts, Mark, I'm injured,' Chris insisted. 'Grandad's seen you play there in practice and rates you. And he should know, he used to be a keeper himself.'

'Yeah, he kept goal for Danebridge Prehistoric United!' giggled Rakesh.

'Well, don't mind where I play,' said Mark. 'If you really want me.'

'Sounds like that's already been decided,' said Mr Jones happily. 'No doubt Chris can lend you all the goalie kit you'll need – and maybe he could take your usual place in midfield. What do you say, Captain?'

Chris couldn't say anything. He was too flabbergasted. He'd never played out on the pitch in a match before in his life!

That evening at home, his brother was almost speechless too – only with laughter – when Chris gave him the team news.

'Glad my own game's been cancelled,' Andrew gasped out at last. 'I wouldn't miss watching this for the world. You in midfield and a girl in attack! Should be hilarious!'

'Don't you come along just to mock. I'm nervous enough as it is.'

'I just can't imagine a girl in a Danebridge shirt,' Andrew snorted in derision. 'Poor old Grandad will have a fit when he finds out.'

'He's already seen how Kerry can score goals. She's wicked!'

'I'll believe it when I see it with my own eyes. Reckon old Jonesy must be cracking up. I wouldn't trust the Professor in goal!'

'And you needn't go trying to put *him* off either during the match,' Chris warned. 'I shall have Grandad on guard duty behind the goal.'

'Never mind him being behind it. If Jonesy was so desperate, I'm surprised he didn't even ask Grandad to play in *front* of it tomorrow!'

In the changing hut on the recky next morning, Chris watched Mark pull on the school's green goalkeeping jersey and felt a sudden pang of resentment. He hadn't envied Mark his promised millions earlier in the week, but having the treasured top now was a different matter. Chris tended to regard it as his own property.

'Don't go playing *too* well, Professor,' he said, managing a smile. 'Remember it's only on loan for the day.'

Mark grinned and stepped into Rakesh's spare tracksuit bottoms. He'd forgotten to bring his own, of course. He also had to make do with the captain's old goalie gloves as Chris was still wearing his new ones. They helped him to feel less strange in a red and white striped shirt.

Chris clapped his gloves together to gain the players' attention before they left the hut. 'OK, men,' he began. 'This is the first round of the cup and we want . . .'

He paused, wondering why everyone was sniggering. Then he realized. Kerry was standing at the back of the group, hands on hips, giving him a hard stare. She had arrived at the hut fully changed and wasn't amused by having to wait outside in the cold until the boys were ready.

'Er . . . sorry, Kerry,' he faltered. 'OK, er . . . team, we want to turn it on today. The cup's our best hope of winning something this season.'

'Yeah, especially now we've missed out on the Lottery!' Mark piped up.

Only he could have got away with saying that in front of Mr Jones. The emergency keeper's joke at his own expense sent the team out in high spirits and their boots clattered down the wooden steps on to the grass.

The ground had fortunately soften-
ed up a little after the mid-week frost,
although the wind was still keen on
any bare flesh. Their opponents,
Brentway Juniors, were smartly
kitted out in royal blue, with
matching gloves, and Kerry immediately felt less conspicuous. She picked
out *two* girls in the Brentway line-up.

So had Andrew. 'There's more of
them!' he exclaimed, shaking his
head. 'What's the game coming to?'

Grandad chuckled. 'You'll have to
get used to it, m'boy. Young Kerry
may be the first girl to play soccer for
Danebridge, but she certainly won't
be the last.'

6 Goals Galore

Chris did not have the best of starts to the game. He lost the toss, let the ball go through his legs to a blue shirt in Brentway's first attack and then watched the girl's shot skid underneath Mark's late dive.

Fortunately for the captain, the ball veered past the wrong side of the post – the right side for Danebridge.

'Had it covered,' Mark claimed with a nervous grin.

Chris and Mark weren't the only

ones with early jitters. Other players were also guilty of uncharacteristic errors, perhaps still unsure about the reliability of their new keeper. Paul showed no confidence in him at all.

After Philip almost headed into his own net, Paul dithered on the ball in front of goal, panicked and gave it away. The free gift was hit hard and true and Mark barely saw it coming. He tried to duck out of the way of the missile, but it smacked him on the

back of his shoulder and spun up and out for a corner. He and Paul exchanged glares and a few words.

Things were little better in attack. Kerry sliced a good chance well wide of the target, staring after the ball in disbelief at her failure to score. And even Rakesh missed a sitter.

'C'mon, Reds!' cried Andrew from the touchline. 'Sort yourselves out. Show them who's boss of the recky!'

That was easier said than done. Brentway had already beaten Danebridge 2-1 at home in the league and now they were seeking a cup double. The visitors pressed hard for the opening goal, forcing Mark to fumble one shot and then deflect a sharp, close-range drive round the post.

'Well saved!' cried Chris, having to

play more in defence than midfield. 'Good job you *did* have that one covered! Would have gone in.'

'If there's one thing I'm good at, it's working out angles,' Mark replied. 'Reckon that was about a thirty degrees acute one. No way was I going to let it sneak in.'

Grandad was pleased too. 'Knew he'd be all right, that lad, once he settled down,' he said to himself. 'He'll be fine now.'

A goal came from the corner, but not for the attacking team. Chris blocked the ball in the six-yard box, Paul hacked it upfield, Kerry helped it on to Rakesh and Danebridge's leading scorer sprinted clear. This time he made no mistake. The break-away goal was against the run of play, but his teammates were not complaining about that.

By half-time, they were all smiles – even Paul. In a flurry of goals before the interval, Rakesh grabbed a second and Brentway responded with a header that Chris himself could not have kept out. But then Kerry stole the show.

She dispossessed one of the Brentway girls outside the area, but found her path to goal barred by two more defenders. She remained ice-cool, shielding the ball skilfully from challenges as she jockeyed for a better shooting position near the penalty spot.

Although passing never seemed to enter her head, Kerry still had her back to goal and looked in need of some help. Suddenly, without warning, she swivelled round and lashed a right-footed shot high into the top corner of the net.

The goalkeeper was left grasping at thin air, caught out by the speed of the strike. It was a moment of sheer class. One that gave proof that here was a natural goalmouth predator.

'Wow!' exclaimed Andrew, despite himself. 'Incredible! I didn't think she had space to do something like that.'

'Neither did they,' chuckled Grandad, looking at the shocked faces of the Brentway side as Danebridge celebrated.

'That's more like it,' Mr Jones encouraged them as the players gathered together at the break. 'You've just about earned this lead after a dodgy start. Three excellent goals and I'm sure there's more to come.'

He was right. Danebridge began the second half in determined fashion. Chris won the ball in the centre-circle, putting in the kind of

powerful tackle that his big brother might have been proud of. He stayed on his feet and sent Rakesh scampering away down the wing with a defence-splitting pass. The winger's cross was met perfectly by Ryan, brought on as substitute again, and he scored his second goal in two games.

There was no stopping Danebridge after that. The football traffic became one-way, streaming towards the Brentway goal like racing cars along the home straight in a Formula One Grand Prix.

Chris was even starting to enjoy himself in midfield. The captain had spent most of the game in his own half so far, battling away to try and break up the visitors' attacks, but now he felt able to join in the fun. Pushing forward deep into Brentway territory, he linked up neatly with Kerry in a move that ended with Rakesh completing his hat-trick.

Rakesh was running riot. He soon added a fourth to double his personal tally for the season, and then curled over a ball for the lanky Philip to climb above everybody else and head into the goal.

'Seven-one!' breathed Grandad. 'They're playing like millionaires!'

'I think you might have put that a bit better!' laughed Andrew, making Grandad redden slightly as he realized what he'd said.

Only once did Brentway manage to turn the tide and remind Mark that he was still playing in the match. On a rare raid, their left-winger swung an awkward cross into the goalmouth, the ball swirling about in the wind. Mark adjusted his position, timed his jump well and caught the ball cleanly, showing a safe pair of hands.

As the opponents retreated, he allowed himself the luxury of bringing his feet into the action too. He dribbled the ball forward, well beyond his own penalty area, before finally hoofing it right into the other one.

The ball was only half-cleared by Brentway, bobbling loose in the box, and Kerry the killer pounced on her prey like a tigress. In a blink of an eye, the ball was nestling once more in the back of the net.

The visitors seemed to give up at last, overwhelmed by the onslaught, and the Danebridge captain put the icing on the cake. Chris, by his own admission, was not exactly 'Man of the Match' – if Kerry and the other girl players would accept such a term – but he deserved some reward for all his hard work. Rakesh was again the unselfish provider.

The winger could quite comfortably have scored a fifth himself, but he slipped the ball square instead to the unmarked Chris who had charged up in support of the attack. Chris hadn't anticipated a pass and for one awful moment, he thought the goalie was going to save his scuffed shot. The ball just trundled beyond his dive and clipped the post on its way in.

'About time, too,' Kerry laughed as Chris looked stunned by his goal. 'I thought you were going to leave all the scoring to us. I hope you've remembered our bet.'

'Giddy-up!' he whooped and slapped an imaginary horse before galloping all the way back to the halfway line. Only Grandad among the spectators could guess the reason for such a bizarre goal-celebration!

'C'mon, let's have double figures!' shouted Andrew, starting up a touch-line chant of 'We want ten!' from the younger supporters.

The team duly obliged. As Mr Jones checked his watch inside the final minute, he looked up to see the strange sight of a green top mixing with the red stripes on yet another Danebridge attack.

'Get back in goal,' Chris called out. 'What are you doing up here?'

'I'm bored!' Mark yelled. 'Got

nothing to do. I just wanted to have a run round and warm up a bit.'

His unexpected arrival in the opposition penalty area threw what was left of Brentway's defensive organization into total chaos. They had no idea who to mark.

Ryan lobbed the ball into the crowded goalmouth and it zigzagged about in a frantic scramble as if in a pinball machine. Both Rakesh and Kerry had efforts blocked before the ball fell invitingly at the feet of the goalkeeper – Danebridge's keeper.

Mark thundered his shot past the helpless Brentway goalie and leapt into the air with delight. It was his first goal of the season. It also gave his team an amazing 10-1 victory.

'This is the best kind of big win!'

Chris cried in excitement. 'Something money just can't buy!'

'Dead right,' Mark agreed happily. 'A nice round number like ten is better than square numbers any day!'

THE END

THE BIG FIX

ROB CHILDS
THE BIG FIX

Illustrated by Aidan Potts

YOUNG CORGI BOOKS

Especially for all referees!

1 Referee!

'Offside, ref!'

The goalkeeper's loud appeal was ignored. So, too, were the claims from the other Danebridge defenders. Their arms were raised in vain.

'Play on!' bellowed the referee.

They had no choice. Nor did they have any hope of catching the Shenby winger. Matthew cut inside for goal, looking to increase his team's lead. Only the keeper barred his way.

But that keeper was Chris Weston,

the Danebridge captain, who also wore the number 1 jersey for the Area side. Chris raced off his line, forcing Matthew to make a hasty decision. To shoot or to dribble.

He shot. He tried to place the ball wide of the onrushing keeper, but Chris's speedy advance narrowed the gap too quickly. The save was top class, straight out of the coaching manual. Chris stayed on his feet until the last moment, then spread his body and blocked the shot with his outstretched leg. The ball cannoned away to safety.

'Great stop!' cried Philip, the Danebridge centre-back. 'They didn't deserve to score. He was miles offside.'

Philip didn't care if his remarks got him into trouble with the referee. He was still cross about Shenby's first 'goal'. The winger had clearly controlled the ball with his hand before shooting.

The home school's referee, their sports teacher, had turned a blind eye to the offence. What made it even harder to take was the brief exchange of words overheard between the referee and the scorer.

'Good goal, Matt, well taken.'

'Thanks, Dad.'

The result of this match meant more than usual to the players involved. Not only was it a local derby between the primary schools of neighbouring villages, but it was also a second round cup-tie.

Danebridge had spent most of the game so far pressed back on defence, but Chris knew there wasn't long to go now until half-time.

'Just hope we can hold out,' he muttered under his breath. 'It's no

thanks to this ref we're only losing one–nil.'

The main thanks, in fact, were due to the captain himself. Even before Shenby had scored their controversial goal, Chris had twice frustrated them with superb saves. A point-blank header had been tipped over the crossbar, and this was followed by a spectacular catch from a deflected shot.

'Here they come again,' Chris groaned as Shenby attacked once more up the right wing.

Jordan, the left-back, missed his tackle and Matthew had plenty of time and space to pick out a target for his centre. He dallied too long, spoilt for

choice, and Jordan recovered well to have a second bite.

Over Matthew went, toppling to the ground like a chopped-down tree. The referee whistled immediately and pointed to the penalty spot.

'I won the ball,' cried Jordan. 'I never even touched him.'

'Foul challenge from behind,' said the referee sternly. 'No arguing.'

Matthew smirked at the goalkeeper

as he placed the ball on the spot, but Chris didn't respond. He was totally focused on the job in hand – trying to keep the ball out of his net.

'OK, son, when you're ready,' said his father.

Matthew ran in and blasted the ball, relying solely on power to do the trick. It worked. Chris dived to his left, but the ball went dead straight – right where he'd been standing.

He lay on the ground, cursing his luck. 'If I'd stayed where I was, I'd have swallowed it.'

Chris's grandad was watching, dismayed, from the touchline. He was the school team's biggest fan and rarely missed a game, home or away.

'This is one of the worst examples of biased refereeing I've ever seen,' he said to Mr Jones, Danebridge's headmaster. 'This chap's far too keen for his own side to win. Who is he?'

The headmaster sighed. 'A new teacher of theirs called Mr Walters. He only started here this term.'

Chris led the complaints as his teammates gathered together at half-time. 'The ref ought to be wearing a blue shirt like his son.'

'Yeah, that kid of his took a dive,' insisted Jordan.

'Bet they practise diving in drama

lessons here,' Philip sneered.

Mr Jones was annoyed himself at some of the referee's decisions, but tried hard not to let it show to the players.

'I know it can be difficult at times, lads,' he said sympathetically, 'but remember that old saying in football: the referee is always right – even when he's wrong.'

2 Cut Short

Danebridge and Shenby had both
made a promising start to the season.
The two schools were riding high in the
league table and also looking forward
to a good cup run. One of them,
however, was in for a disappointment.

Midway through the second half, the
visitors' chances of being in the next
round appeared slim. Danebridge
were still trailing 2–0 to a team that
could do no wrong in the eyes of the
referee.

Fouls by Shenby continued to go unpunished and free-kicks were awarded in their favour at every opportunity. Often the players had no idea why they had been penalized.

'I don't believe this guy!' Philip muttered as Mr Walters gave another corner instead of a goal-kick after the ball came off a Shenby knee.

'Good job Pud's not here,' said Jordan. 'He'd be going ballistic!'

Mr Jones, too, was relieved about the absence of their usual number nine. He guessed Pud's short temper would have blown a fuse by now and made matters far worse. Danebridge might have been reduced to ten men.

'Mark up tight, defence,' shouted Chris as Matthew prepared to take the corner. 'Get to the ball first.'

Philip made sure he did just that. His height was a great advantage at set-pieces. He rose well above friend and foe alike to head the ball firmly away out of danger. It dropped at the feet of Jamie Robertson, Danebridge's wizard of the dribble.

Freckle-faced Jamie may have been the baby of the team in terms of age, but he was their most skilful player. The little winger had had very few touches of the ball up to this moment and now meant to keep it to himself. There was nothing he enjoyed more than a long solo dribble.

Jamie scampered off along the touchline, drawing opponents towards him like moths to a flame. They closed in, one behind the other for extra

cover, as if queuing up to be mesmer-
ized by his dazzling footwork.

'He's up to his tricks again,' laughed
Jordan. 'We might as well all have a sit
down for a bit till he gets tired.'

Jamie pranced and danced his way
past most of the bewildered defenders,
but in the end, he overdid it – as usual.
Trying one trick too many, he beat
himself rather than had the ball taken
off him. It bobbled loose in the penalty
area and was hastily hacked away.

Not very far. The miskicked clearance went to the only Danebridge player who had followed up Jamie's run. Ryan was lurking on the edge of the area, just inside the 'D'. He took one touch to control the ball and then one more to drive it low past the keeper into the net.

There was no doubt that Pud's strength and power had been missed in attack, but not even he could have hit the shot any better than Ryan. Nor could the referee find an excuse to disallow such a well-struck goal.

'That was sloppy defending,' cried Mr Walters. 'Wake up!'

Shenby were jolted into action as if their alarm clock had just gone off. They bombarded Chris's goal with shots and crosses, and Danebridge could barely get the ball out of their own half. Something had to give.

No-one could complain about Shenby's third goal. Dominic, their captain, deserved the credit for it, bursting through a gap into a good scoring position himself. He feinted to shoot, wrong-footing Chris, then unselfishly switched the ball to the unmarked Matthew. The winger only had to tap it over the line to complete his hat-trick.

At 3–1, the cup-tie seemed to be settled, but Mr Jones knew that his team would never give up. He glanced at his watch – and so did Grandad.

'Still got time,' Grandad called out. 'C'mon, you can do it, Reds.'

Shenby were caught dozing again. They had relaxed their guard after scoring and paid the price. The red and white striped shirts of Danebridge sliced through their casual defence and Jamie dribbled round the goalkeeper to finish off the move in style.

'Oh dear, they'll be for it on Monday morning,' chuckled Grandad, seeing the referee's furious expression. 'Let's hope for their sakes that he cools down over the weekend.'

Mr Jones studied his watch again. 'A couple of minutes left at least,' he said. 'We might snatch a replay yet.'

But as Danebridge regained possession from the restart and Ryan sprinted forward with the ball, a long, shrill blast rent the air.

'Full-time!' the referee called out. 'Shenby win 3–2.'

'Never! He's gone and blown early,' exclaimed Grandad. 'What a rotten thing to do!'

The substitutes nearby heard Grandad's remark and were quick to tell their teammates what had

happened. They felt cheated. Chris always made a point, as captain, of shaking the referee's hand after the match, but not on this occasion. He deliberately snubbed him.

Dominic came to slump next to Chris as he removed his muddy boots outside the cloakroom. 'Soz about the ref. I know how you must be feeling,' he began. 'We're fed up with him too. He spoils our games.'

'Really?' grunted Chris, standing up.

'So what are you going to do about it? I didn't hear any of you objecting when he gave that penalty.'

*

On the way home, Chris, Philip and Jordan sat together in the back of Grandad's car. It was a quiet journey. The full shock of Danebridge's early exit from the cup was taking some time to sink in.

'Can't wait till we meet them in the league,' said Jordan as they stopped by his house. 'It'll be a real grudge match.'

'Yeah, revenge is sweet!' muttered Philip.

'Just hope it's at home so we don't have to suffer their ref again,' Chris said, and saw Grandad frown.

'I'm afraid not, m'boy. Mr Jones told me we're due back at their place in a fortnight's time!'

Grandad dropped Philip off too before he spoke his mind to Chris. 'I reckon it might not be a bad idea for Mr Jones to postpone that league game. Y'know, give things a bit longer to blow over.'

Chris pulled a face. 'It'd look as if we're wimps or something, too scared to play them.'

Grandad sighed. 'Well, if it does go ahead, it'll be up to you to lead by example.'

'How do you mean?'

'It's always important to play the game in the right spirit, no matter what, and you must spell that out to your team. They'll listen to you – even hotheads like that Pud. You've got their respect.'

'But it made me so mad as well today.'

'Aye, maybe, but you can't play football properly if you lose your temper. Cool heads, that's what it's going to take to outwit that ref and beat his team fair and square.'

3 Gunpowder Plot

It wasn't only Pud who perhaps lacked a cool head, especially on Bonfire Night. Philip and Jordan were standing rather too close to the heat of the roaring bonfire on the village recreation ground.

They were both still grumbling about the Shenby defeat.

'Reckon it was all a big fix from the start,' Jordan sneered.

Philip nodded as he munched on a hot dog. 'Yeah, now we know why

games are sometimes called *fixtures*!'

They watched a rocket whoosh up into the dark sky and explode in a brief, bright flare of coloured lights.

'Right, but somehow we'll have to make sure that ref doesn't get away with it again in the league match,' said Jordan.

Mustard dribbled down Philip's chin and he wiped it off with the sleeve of his jacket. 'Well, Pud will be back in the team then,' he spluttered. 'He won't stand for any sort of nonsense.'

Jordan pointed Pud out near the hot-dog stand. 'Look, he's over there, stuffing himself silly as usual. He's got food in both paws.'

'Said he was off school with an upset stomach,' Philip grinned. 'Not surprised. If I were his stomach, I'd be upset too!'

'Look who's talking, the amount of

grub you've put away this evening.'

'I'm a growing lad.'

'It's about time you stopped. If you grow any taller, you'll be more use at netball than football.'

'Don't you mean basketball?'

'No, netball. If the girls fastened a net round your head, they could use you as a post for shooting practice!'

Another cascade of lights burst over the crowd enjoying the firework display. But what made Chris suddenly jump was the thump of a heavy hand on his shoulder. He hadn't seen Andrew sneak up on him from behind.

'Bet I know who you'd like to see

on top of that bonfire instead of poor old Guy Fawkes, eh, little brother?' Andrew sniggered.

A number of people, including Andrew, sprang instantly to mind. Chris hated being called little brother. Although he was two years younger, he was rapidly catching up in height.

'Wally!' Andrew cackled. 'That's what the Shenby lot call that Walters bloke you've been droning on about all week.'

'How do you know that?'

''Cos my pal here told me. Gaz, come and meet my little brother.'

The youth strolled across to them, a can of cola in his hand. He took a long swig as he sized Chris up.

'So you're this keeper that my own kid brother reckons stopped them scoring double figures?'

'Come off it,' Chris snorted. 'It wasn't

that one-sided. Shenby were hanging on at the end, despite all the ref's cheating. Who is your brother, anyway?'

'Dominic,' he smirked.

Chris turned on Andrew. 'You didn't tell me you knew their captain's brother.'

'You never asked. Gaz is a good mate of mine at school. We're both gonna come and watch your league match at

Shenby. We want to see this Wally in action.'

Chris groaned. 'There's probably going to be enough bother as it is. You two won't exactly help the situation.'

'Ah, but that's where you're wrong, our kid,' Andrew began before being interrupted by a series of deafening bangs. 'If things go to plan, it sounds like you can expect a few fireworks that day as well . . .'

*

'Now we're out of the cup, we can concentrate on the league,' said Ryan during a lunchtime soccer practice. 'At least we can still win that.'

'Dead right,' grunted Pud. 'League's more important, in any case. Proves who's the best team over the whole season.'

Pud was fit again. Or as fit as he was ever going to be. He carried too much

bulk around his middle to have a chance of outrunning anybody. He didn't need to. He tripped them up instead before they could run away.

'We missed you against Shenby,' said Ryan.

Pud beamed, flattered by the compliment, until Jamie piped up.

'Yeah, you being away sure left a big hole in the team!'

'Watch it, Gingernut,' Pud growled, assuming Jamie was trying to be cheeky as usual. They enjoyed trading insults with each other.

Mr Jones interrupted the banter. 'Come on, let's see some action there. I want you three to sharpen up your shooting boots for Saturday.'

Danebridge had another league match to play at home first before they renewed their battle with Shenby. As the visitors were bottom of the table, the boys saw it as a golden opportunity to boost their goal tally.

Especially Pud. His cannonball shooting was a threat to the health and safety of any goalkeeper.

'I'm gonna fill my boots against Eastgate,' he boasted.

Jamie grinned. 'Reckon you fill them pretty good already. Your feet are massive.'

'What I mean, Clever Dick, is that I'm gonna score ten goals.'

'About the only time you'll ever count to ten!'

Pud was riled and suddenly lashed a ball goalwards. Chris wasn't even ready and it was only his quick reflexes that saved him from decapitation. He saw the ball at the last moment and ducked his head out of the way a split second before he might have had it knocked off.

He gave Pud a hard stare. 'No need to guess who hit that one. Go back a bit, will you. You're too close.'

The three strikers kept Chris busy during the shooting practice. They looked on good form, and so did Chris, but he was grateful they were using small-sized goals.

It took a very good shot indeed to beat him and Pud produced it. He

connected with a short pass from Ryan
so sweetly that the ball seemed to
gather pace as it flashed through the
air and into the net. It barely rose off
the ground, leaving Chris flailing in its
slipstream.

'Almost broke the land speed record
there, Big Fellow,' Jamie praised him
to get back into Pud's good books for a
while.

At the end of the session, Mr Jones
named the team to play Eastgate.
'Don't take it for granted that you'll
have an easy win,' he warned them.
'Anything can happen in football. It's a
funny old game, as they say.'

He didn't hear Philip muttering at the back of the group.

'Huh! They wouldn't have said that if they'd come up against Wally. There isn't much to laugh about when *he's* blowing his whistle.'

4 Put to the Test

Next morning, the footballers of
Danebridge did not find the start of
their game at all amusing. Eastgate
opened the scoring in the very first
minute. Or at least that's what the
referee decided.

Chris took the sting out of a fierce
shot but was helpless to prevent the
ball rolling towards the net. To his
relief, Jordan managed to scramble
back in time, stretch out a foot and
hook the ball away.

'Thanks, great covering,' cried Chris as the visitors claimed a goal.

'That was in, ref,' came a shout from the touchline.

'Ball went over the line,' insisted their number eight. 'I saw it.'

Mr Jones, the referee, hesitated a moment and then made up his mind. He pointed to the centre-circle and the Eastgate team danced away in celebration. His own players were left

gaping. No-one actually dared to say anything, but he guessed what they were thinking.

'Hard to tell whether or not the whole ball had crossed the line before Jordan got a boot to it,' Mr Jones explained, half apologetically. 'I had to give Eastgate the benefit of the doubt. That's only fair.'

'*Fair*, he says!' Philip snorted as soon as the headmaster was out of earshot. 'After what happened to us last Saturday!'

'That's probably why he favoured them,' sighed Chris. 'Nothing we can do about it now apart from try and equalize.'

That was easier said than done. For a while, it seemed to be one of those days when the ball simply refused to go in the net. Danebridge were dominating the game, but chance after chance went begging. Pud miskicked in front of an open goal, Ryan fired another sitter over the bar and Jamie dribbled himself dizzy in ever-decreasing circles.

And when they did get any shots on target, the ball flew straight into the Eastgate goalkeeper's gloves like a well-trained homing pigeon.

Only as the seconds ticked away towards the break did Danebridge finally succeed. Even then, they needed a helping hand – or head. Ryan floated in a harmless-looking cross into the goalmouth and a defender panicked. He heard the pounding of heavy feet behind him and headed the

ball under the bar instead of over it as he tried to clear.

'The kid had to play the ball,' said Pud during the half-time team-talk. 'He knew I was right behind him if he left it.'

'I bet he did,' grinned Jamie. 'He must have thought he was going to get flattened by a runaway elephant!'

It was a good job for Jamie that Pud was in a better mood after the embarrassment of his earlier miss. And that Mr Jones stood between them.

'It's just a matter of time now,' said the headmaster. 'Be patient. Keep playing the way you are, making chances, and the goals will come.'

He was right. Chris hardly had a touch of the ball in the second half as Danebridge clicked into top gear. He was as much of a spectator as Grandad who was standing on the touchline with Shoot, their border collie.

Chris enjoyed the dog's reactions every time a goal was scored. Shoot joined in with the antics of the excited people around them, jumping up at Grandad and barking madly, not sure what all the fuss was about. He preferred chasing cats and sticks to watching football matches.

After Jamie put Danebridge ahead from Ryan's pass, the goalie's pigeons must have fled the loft. The two wingers ran riot, scoring two goals each, before Jamie set Pud up for the sixth and final strike.

Jamie saw Pud in space outside the penalty area and surprised everyone by passing the ball to him. 'All yours, Big Fellow,' he called out.

Pud was desperate to add his own name to the scoresheet that Mr Jones always put on the sports noticeboard after a game. He hammered the ball with all his might and the goalie made sure he wasn't in the way of the thunderbolt. He didn't want to go

home himself with dislocated fingers.

'Six of the best!' cried Philip. 'Watch out, Wally, here we come!'

On the following Friday, at morning break, Chris called a private team meeting in a sheltered corner of the windy playground.

'If we want to be champions this season, we can't afford to lose to Shenby again,' he stressed, 'but . . .'

He was immediately interrupted. 'Right, but we're playing against twelve men,' said Philip. 'Them and their ref.'

'Yeah, looks like we'll have to make them use a sub,' Pud smirked. 'If I collided with Wally, sort of accidentally on purpose, he might have to be carried off. Jonesy could take over then.'

'He'd probably give them more goals

than Wally,' Jordan scoffed.

Chris brought the meeting to order. 'Look, I've said we need to win, but it's got to be done in the right way. If we let Wally rattle us, we've had it. We've got to keep our heads and play it cool.'

The captain could see that some of the team were not yet convinced and he wanted to make sure his message was taken seriously.

'Jonesy very nearly called this match off, you know, but I reckon he's testing us instead,' Chris continued. 'If we show any dissent to Wally, he might even stop the game and hand the points to Shenby. Just imagine how we'd feel then.'

'So what are we gonna do?' said Jordan. 'Let them walk all over us?'

'No way!' Pud muttered. 'Nobody walks over me.'

'Quicker than trying to walk round you,' Jamie quipped.

Chris put a restraining hand on Pud's arm as the striker made a move towards the joker.

'We've *all* got to pass Jonesy's test –

including you, Pud. One flash of your temper against the ref and we could be on our way home early. And that could be the last time you'll ever play for the school . . .'

Chris confessed his worries about the game to Andrew when he got home that afternoon. 'Are you still thinking of coming with us to watch?'

'No – I'll already be there.' Andrew grinned at his brother's puzzled face. 'Didn't I tell you? I'm staying over at Gaz's place tonight. Nice and handy then for the big match in the morning.'

'Look, I don't really care if you're there or not, but please don't do anything to show us up, OK?'

'As if I would,' Andrew said, the picture of innocence. 'We're just gonna fix a few things with Dominic for tomorrow, that's all.'

'What d'yer mean by that?' Chris

said gruffly. 'Stay out of it, will you. We had enough fixing going on last time.'

'Relax, our kid, no need to lose any sleep over it,' Andrew chuckled. 'Well, can't stand here chatting all day. Must pack my bag. Got places to go, people to see . . .'

Chris feared the worst. He was in for a restless night.

5 *Nightmare Game*

Chris stared at the football in dismay. It sat in the back of the net, mocking him as he lay in a pool of muddy water. Beaten yet again.

He'd lost count of the score. It must have been about 10–0 to Shenby. He reckoned half the goals were offside, two should have been ruled out for handball and Chris had saved another of them before it crossed the line. But Wally awarded a goal every single time.

Now Matthew had just scored from a penalty for a foul by Philip outside the area. And to make matters even worse, Wally had gone and sent Philip off. He'd already given Pud his marching orders.

Chris staggered to his feet and glanced towards Grandad to seek some advice about what to do. He could hardly believe his eyes. Grandad was invading the pitch, waving his fists at the referee.

Nobody else seemed to have noticed. Pud was too busy kicking Matthew until his victim sank to his knees and cried out for mercy.

Chris tried to cut Grandad off, but his legs felt like lead weights. He wasn't able to get there in time. Then Andrew rode on to the pitch on his bike. He reached the referee first and punched the teacher himself. Wally toppled to the ground, blood pouring from his nose.

The whole playing field had become a chaotic free-for-all. Fights had broken out between the two sets of players and among the parents on the touchline. Even Shoot was involved, barking and snarling at people. Chris couldn't understand why Mr Jones was doing nothing to stop it. He was just standing in the centre-circle and laughing.

Chris screamed and then put his fingers into his mouth to give a loud whistle, hoping it would make everybody come to their senses . . .

He woke up in a cold sweat. It was still dark. He didn't know where he was until a door opened and let in a stream of light. A dog also bounded in and began licking at his face.

'What on earth is all that noise about?' asked Mum, pulling Shoot away. 'Are you all right? You've been screaming and whistling.'

Chris looked around the bedroom in a daze, still trying to gather his wits. It had all seemed so very real.

'Sorry, Mum,' he said lamely. 'Must have been having a bad dream.'

'I'll say it was. You've kicked all your bedclothes on to the floor and it looks like you've been fighting with your pillow.'

Chris gazed at the devastated bed and grinned. 'Just practising for the match. We're gonna sort Shenby out.'

'Well, you can sort your bed out first,' she said. 'At least you haven't gone and wet it!'

'Aw, Mum!' he said in disgust. 'You know I never do that. A good goalie always keeps clean sheets!'

*

Chris emerged from the Shenby school cloakroom to spot Andrew against the fence on the far side of the pitch. Gaz

and Dominic were there too, surrounded by a bunch of blue shirts. The discussions looked to be pretty lively with lots of arm-waving.

'Wonder what that's all about?' he mused, suspiciously.

As Chris went across to investigate, the group broke up and most of the Shenby players drifted away. A white-faced Matthew was among them.

'Hiya, little brother,' Andrew greeted him cheerily. 'Bet you missed me last night. Sleep well?'

'Not exactly,' Chris muttered. 'Had things on my mind.'

'Told you, Gaz. Always a worrier, our kid. That's why I have to help him out at times.'

'I can do without your kind of help,' said Chris, thinking of his nightmarish battlefield. He was glad Andrew didn't have his bike with him.

'Huh! That's all the thanks we get for trying to do him a favour.'

'Typical!' Gaz joined in. 'We'll see if he changes his tune later on.'

They sauntered off, sniggering,

138

leaving the two captains staring at each other awkwardly.

'Something's going on, isn't it?' said Chris. 'What's the big secret?'

'Nothing,' Dominic replied, glancing round nervously. 'Well, nothing I can let on about right now. You'll find out soon enough when it happens . . . *if* it happens.'

'If *what* happens?' persisted Chris, anxious to get to the bottom of the mystery. 'Are our brothers behind all this?'

'No, it's a kind of team effort, really – but it was you who first put the idea into my head after the cup match.'

Chris was stunned. 'Me? How?'

'Soz, got to go and speak to someone,' said Dominic, avoiding the questions. He ran off to catch Matthew up and Chris saw him take the number seven to one side for a private talk.

The Danebridge captain gave a shrug and went to inspect the pitch, which was soggy and slippery after the overnight rain. When he reached one of the goalmouths, he suddenly realized there were no nets on the posts. Nor on those at the other end. His teammates had already noticed.

'Gives Wally a better chance of pulling a fast one,' growled Philip.

'How d'yer mean?' asked Ryan. 'It's the same for both sides.'

'Not with Wally as ref, it isn't. He's up to something, I bet.'

'He's not the only one either,' Chris murmured under his breath.

The match began ominously for Danebridge. Pud was penalized twice in the opening minutes, once for pushing and then for scoring. He beat the Shenby goalkeeper with a powerful drive from the edge of the penalty area, but his delight quickly gave way to amazement.

'No goal!' announced the referee. 'Offside.'

'I wasn't offside,' Pud protested.

Mr Walters glared at him. 'Your number eleven was in an offside position when you shot.'

'He wasn't interfering with play.'

'Don't argue with me, lad. I've made a decision. No goal.'

While the goalkeeper fetched the ball, Pud stood fuming in frustration, hands on hips. Steam almost seemed to be coming out of his ears.

'Sorry, Big Fellow,' said Jamie. 'Must have strayed too far forward.'

'Not your fault – for once,' Pud muttered. 'That cheat was just using you as an excuse.'

'Not sure I like the look of this,' remarked Grandad. 'Things might get a bit out of hand here soon.'

Mr Jones nodded. 'I'm beginning to wish that I'd followed my better judgement and cancelled this game.'

'Too late now, I'm afraid. We'll just have to keep our fingers crossed and hope for the best.'

Luck was certainly with Danebridge a minute later when they enjoyed a let-off themselves. Matthew swivelled and hit a snapshot on the turn beyond Chris's reach, but the ball smacked against the top of the post and rebounded back into play.

'Surprised the ref didn't say the ball crossed the line,' said Jordan sarcastically after Philip cleared the danger. 'Especially as it was his precious son.'

'Give him time. Don't touch Matthew inside the area whatever you do. Even shaking his hand would earn them a penalty.'

'How about shaking him by the throat?'

Philip grinned. 'Only when the ref's not looking.'

Shenby were a good enough side in their own right not to need any extra help from the referee. He was determined, however, to give it to them. The favouritism he showed was so blatant that even the Shenby parents began to laugh at his bizarre decisions in order to hide their embarrassment. The Danebridge supporters felt more like crying.

It came as a total shock to everyone, therefore, when Danebridge broke away to score and the goal was allowed to stand.

6 Like Father, Like Son?

The Shenby goalkeeper hung his head in shame.

Jamie's hopeful cross from the left wing had plopped straight into his arms – and out again. The wet ball was like a bar of soap in the bath, and he'd let it slip out of his grasp and over the line.

As a former goalie, Grandad couldn't help feeling a little sorry for the boy. 'I think he was wise not to try and catch

the ref's eye,' he chuckled to himself. 'Just in case he went and dropped that too!'

Inside two minutes, however, the goalkeeper's mistake was cancelled out by Matthew's volley. But the only person who saw it as an equalizing goal was the one in charge – the referee.

Chris had the shot well covered, diving to make sure the ball couldn't squeeze between him and the post. He was horrified when he realized the referee had given a goal. Even Matthew looked astonished by the decision and turned away, showing no pleasure in scoring. He knew he hadn't.

'That went wide!' Chris protested. 'Would have hit the side netting.'

'Not from my angle,' said Mr Walters. 'The goal stands. One–all.'

A loud cry rang out over the playing field. 'What a wally! You're not even any good at cheating, ref!'

The furious referee scanned the touchline for the culprit, without success. Chris knew who it was of course. He picked out Andrew peering from behind the shelter of a tree.

At half-time, the Danebridge players were still angry at the injustice of the goal and had never seen their headmaster so upset.

'Bet Jonesy won't say anything today about the ref always being right!' muttered Philip.

Their attention was caught by raised voices from the Shenby group some distance away. A few of the boys' parents seemed to be making their feelings known to Mr Walters very strongly.

'He's got a revolt on his hands, by the look of it,' said Mr Jones. 'Deserves it too, the way he's been acting.'

'I always said that Shenby were revolting,' grinned Pud.

'C'mon, team,' Chris rallied them as they took up their positions for the delayed second half. 'They're bound to be a bit shaken up for a while after all that arguing. Let's get at 'em. We can still win this game.'

They did their best to follow the captain's instructions. Both Jamie and Ryan had shots on target, but each time the keeper was equal to the task. He was careful to position his body right behind the line of the ball and the two saves helped to restore his confidence.

To their credit, Shenby settled down and hit back, giving as good as they got. A firm header brought Chris into action, too, alert as ever to any danger. He was grateful, though, to see a powerful, swirling shot clip

Philip on the shoulder and deflect safely over the crossbar.

'Handball! Penalty kick,' announced the referee, to the disbelief of everybody, on and off the pitch. 'You take it, Matthew.'

'But it was nowhere near his hand, Dad.'

'Don't *you* start now. Just do as you're told, lad.'

There were boos coming from the touchline, and not just from Andrew and other Danebridge supporters. Many of the Shenby people were joining in too.

Matthew was visibly trembling as he placed the ball on the penalty spot. He turned and glanced at Dominic on the edge of the area in a silent, desperate appeal for help. The captain sensed that his teammate might not have the nerve to carry out the agreed plan.

Gaz doubted it too. He made a strange sight by the corner flag. He was frantically waving his brother forward, miming a kick at an imaginary ball.

As Matthew took several steps back and the whistle sounded, Dominic suddenly brushed past him. Chris was taken by surprise but didn't need to bother diving. Dominic scooped the ball almost comically high over the bar, as if he'd done it on purpose.

The cheers and laughter died away as the referee insisted the penalty be retaken. 'Doesn't count. You can't switch kickers at the last moment like that,' he declared, bending the rules to his own advantage.

'I don't mind – he missed,' said Chris. 'It should be a goal-kick.'

Mr Walters ignored him and grabbed Dominic by the arm. 'I don't know what you think you're playing at,' he hissed. 'I'll deal with you later.'

Dominic shrugged, pulled himself free and gave Matthew a little nod of encouragement as they passed each other. 'Go on, Matt, you can do it,' the captain urged. 'Show him how we all feel.'

Matthew replaced the ball and looked up at Chris. 'Just stay where you are,' he said, forcing a sickly grin.

Chris was confused. He thought Matthew must be trying to taunt him, but the boy looked in no mood for playing any tricks.

Matthew moved in, but slowed as he neared the ball and simply tapped it along the ground straight at the keeper. The ball barely reached him. All Chris had to do was bend down and pick it up.

Mr Walters stared open-mouthed at his son.

'Sorry, Dad, I just didn't think it was fair to score . . .'

Matthew dried up, his face deathly pale as he waited for his father to erupt. But the explosion never came.

The spark had gone out.

The rest of the Shenby team gathered around to support Matthew and Dominic. The captain gulped, took a deep breath, and then spoke up. He'd been rehearsing what to say with Gaz and Andrew.

'We want to win as much as anybody, Mr Walters, but not at all costs. It's not right. We don't like people thinking we're cheats.'

The teacher nodded dumbly, not knowing how to respond. Then he turned on his heel, trudged across to Mr Jones and offered him the whistle.

'Sorry I've been such a fool. I realize that now, thanks to these lads, and I feel ashamed of myself. Please take over from me.'

The headmaster shook his head. 'I'm hardly dressed for the part,' he smiled, pointing at his wellies. 'You carry on. It won't do any harm for the boys to see that teachers can learn their lessons too.'

Mr Walters, duly humbled, repeated his apologies to the players. 'I'll award you the game, if you like,' he said to the

Danebridge team. 'It might make up a little for the cup match.'

'No need for that,' Chris replied. 'Like Dominic, all we want is a fair contest – win, lose or draw.'

'Right, so let's get this ball rolling again,' said the referee. 'Score's still one–all – and may the best team win.'

The game was played in a strange atmosphere for the next few minutes as the footballers tried to pick up the momentum. For the Shenby boys, it felt almost like an anti-climax after the success of their revolution.

Dominic brought the match back to life when he tested Chris's reflexes from close-range. The opposing captain blocked the shot and dived on the rebound before Dominic could follow it up.

'This is more like it, eh?' said Dominic, helping Chris to his feet.

'Yeah, better late than never,' he grinned.

Both goalies were kept busy for the remaining minutes of the game. Shenby's had his hands warmed by Jordan's rocket and also held on to a looping header from Philip that was destined for the top corner.

Matthew had been understandably subdued since the penalty incident, but perked up when given the chance to run with the ball. He almost twisted Jordan inside-out with a skilful dribble down the wing, creating space for a shot that Chris only smothered at the second attempt.

'Well played, son, great effort,' his dad praised him. 'And well saved, too, keeper.'

What finally convinced Danebridge that the referee had turned over a new leaf was when he blew for offside

against Shenby in the next attack. It was their first free-kick in either game.

And they made it count. It was from Jordan's quick pass to Jamie that Danebridge regained the lead.

Jamie cantered away with the ball up the left wing, riding a couple of challenges like a jockey in a steeplechase race. The going was very soft. He squelched through a large puddle, losing control for a moment, but just managed to squirt the ball across to Pud.

Danebridge's carthorse did the rest. Pud's pent-up feelings were all released in his ferocious whack at the ball. It was one of his special master-blasters. The poor goalkeeper had a long trek to retrieve the ball.

The goal made the score 2–1 and proved to be the winning strike. Mr

Walters didn't dare allow much added time in case Shenby grabbed an equalizer. He didn't want to be accused of playing on until they scored.

Everyone was glad to hear the final whistle and put the match behind them. Chris even went up to shake the referee's hand this time before seeking out Dominic. The two captains were joined in the centre-circle by their older brothers.

'Nice one, Dom!' cried Gaz. 'You did it, kid. Knew you could stand up to that Wally.'

Andrew slapped Dominic on the back. 'The plan worked like a dream.'

'What plan was that exactly?' asked Chris.

'Well, we guessed Wally would give us a penalty we didn't deserve,' explained Dominic. 'We decided that was the best time to have a kind of showdown with him. We should have done it before, like you said.'

'What about Matthew? Bet he took a bit of persuading.'

'Yeah, he did, but it all worked out well in the end.'

'Apart from the fact that you lost,' put in Gaz.

'It was worth it. We've made our point.'

'Looks like all is forgiven, anyway,' said Chris, nodding towards the school. The teacher was walking alongside Matthew, his arm around his son's shoulders. 'Wally ought to be grateful for what you did today.'

'Why's that?'

'For reminding him that cheats never prosper!'

THE END

THE BIG FREEZE

ROB CHILDS
THE BIG FREEZE

Illustrated by Aidan Potts

YOUNG CORGI BOOKS

Especially for Dad –
simply the best!

1 Frozen Up

'Have a crack! Hit it!'

Pud didn't really need any such encouragement – least of all from the goalkeeper in his direct line of fire. If there was one thing Pud was good at, it was hitting a football.

So he hit it – hard. Not quite one of his megapower master-blasters, as teammates at Danebridge Primary School called them, but still fierce enough to send defenders diving for cover.

Chris Weston, team captain and goalie, might have told Pud to shoot, but he wasn't *that* stupid. He made no attempt to block it either. He didn't want to risk injury in a knockabout game in the village hall.

Chris let the ball whistle past him and watched it fly wide of the cone too. 'Close! Bad luck, Pud,' he cried out.

'Good shot, David,' praised Mr Jones, resisting the temptation to use the boy's nickname. 'Always worth a pop at goal from there.'

'I'll have a pop from anywhere,' Pud muttered under his breath, cross that he hadn't scored.

'Take a break now, boys,' the headmaster told them.

Most of the players trooped off for a drink of water, but David Bakewell waddled over to a long wooden bench and slumped against the wall. He was joined by his captain.

'Budge up a bit, Pud.'

'What do you mean by that?' he scowled. 'There's plenty of room, I'm not that fat.'

'I never said you were,' Chris defended himself. 'I just want to get to my bag under the bench.'

Like everyone else, Chris had to be a

little wary of Pud's fiery temper. Nothing lit the striker's short fuse quicker than a remark about his size, intentional or otherwise.

'Want a crisp?' Chris asked as he took a packet out of his sports bag.

'What flavour?'

'Smoky bacon.'

'Right, yeah, thanks,' Pud mumbled, pulling out a podgy handful and stuffing them all into his mouth at the same time.

'Would it have mattered what flavour they were?'

'Not really,' Pud spluttered and then grinned. 'I like 'em all.'

'So I've noticed,' Chris sighed, tucking in himself before Pud fancied any second helpings.

'Just look at Carrot-Top!' snorted

Pud. 'Still dribbling himself daft round all them cones over there.'

They watched little Jamie Robertson waltzing through a line of cones, the ball almost glued to his feet. It wasn't only his red hair that caught the eye. It was his dazzling, twinkle-toed footwork. Despite being two years younger than most of the team, Jamie's speed and tricky ball skills down the wing had produced many of Danebridge's goals so far that season.

The crackly sound of a transistor radio distracted them. 'Huh!' Pud grunted. 'Jonesy stopped the game just to hear the weather forecast!'

'Shut up and listen,' said Chris, hoping for a let-up in the worst winter weather that even his watching grandad could remember.

'The big freeze continues . . .' began

the lady's voice and Chris groaned. It had been the same message for weeks. The deep snow had been fun in the Christmas holidays, but now everywhere was covered with hard-packed ice and he was fed up with all the short, dark, bitterly cold days.

Even worse was the fact that the freezing weather was wrecking their soccer season. It was nearly the end of January and they hadn't played a proper match for two months.

'We're going to have a massive fixture pile-up at this rate.'

'Yeah,' Pud agreed, 'and that won't do our chances of winning the league any good, will it?'

Chris shivered. 'Brrr! It's cold in here tonight too. We should have kept on the move like Jamie.'

'Skinny kids daren't stop or they turn to icicles,' Pud laughed.

Chris went to speak to Grandad. 'No sign of a thaw yet, I gather. By the time we see any grass again, it'll be the cricket season.'

Grandad chuckled. 'Aye, and then it'll probably rain every day!'

When the headmaster restarted the game, Jamie wasted no time in testing out Chris's reflexes. His low, skidding shot took a slight deflection, but the keeper threw himself across the mat to turn the ball away.

'Thought I'd beat you there,' smiled Jamie.

'He wouldn't have smelt it, if I'd whacked it,' Pud boasted. 'Your shots are too weedy.'

Jamie shrugged. 'At least mine are on target!'

The practice continued at half-pace, the novelty of playing indoors having long worn off. The dimly lit, draughty room was far from ideal, but it was the only place they had to keep up their football.

This was why the boys greeted the headmaster's unexpected news at the end of the session with such excitement.

'I know you'll be glad of a change of scene,' he smiled. 'Jamie's father works at the new sports centre in Selworth and he's booked us in for some sessions on the all-weather pitches there.'

'Football under floodlights! Magic!' Chris enthused.

As they collected their coats, Pud collared Jamie. 'Why didn't you tell us earlier about the sports centre, eh, Gingernut?'

'My little secret,' he grinned impishly. 'Wanted it to be a surprise.'

'It sure was that, all right,' laughed Chris. 'What's this astro-turf like to play on, do you know?'

'Wicked! Dead flat, great for dribbling – as long as you've got the right kind of shoes.'

The players nearby looked down at their own feet. 'Aren't ordinary trainers any good?' asked Pud.

'You need special ones with better grip like I've got at home,' Jamie replied. 'Try to turn and shoot in those old things and you'll be flipped over on your back like a helpless tortoise!'

2 Floodlit Football

'Wow!' gasped Chris as Grandad pulled into the sports centre car park. 'Just look at all those lights.'

'Yeah, almost like daytime!' exclaimed Andrew, his elder brother, who had insisted on coming with them. 'Wish I could join in myself.'

Also in the car was Philip Smith, Danebridge's giraffe-like centre-back. 'Can't wait to try out my new trainers,' he babbled. 'Got them yesterday. Dad said I'd be sliding

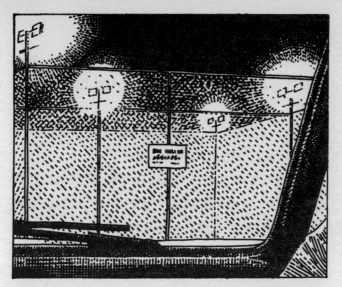

about all over the place otherwise.'

That was the one thing that was bothering Chris, but he tried to put it to the back of his mind. 'Hey! Look who's over there!' he cried as they walked towards the changing rooms. 'You see who I see, Phil?'

'Carl Diamond!' Philip groaned. 'Nobody could miss a head that size.'

'C'mon, he's not that bad, once you get to know him.'

Philip pulled a face. 'He still tries to

act the superstar too much for my liking. And I usually end up having to mark him!'

'Not tonight,' laughed Chris. 'He's with his Highgate squad.'

Andrew broke away from the group. 'Think I'll go and watch him for a bit, OK? While you lot get yourselves sorted out.'

'It wouldn't be because there's some teenage girls playing hockey nearby, would it, Andrew?' Grandad teased him.

'Is there?' he said innocently, colouring up. 'Hadn't even noticed.'

'I bet.' Chris grinned. 'Didn't know you were such a fan of Carl's.'

'I'm not. Just thought he might be able to get Dazzler Diamond's autograph for me. Best player in the

World Cup, his uncle was.'

'You'll be lucky. Probably have to wait till some big club pays millions to tempt him to leave Africa and come to play in this country.'

Philip tugged Chris's arm. 'C'mon, I'll have outgrown my new shoes by the time we get changed.'

As it was such a cold evening, Mr Jones organized a vigorous warm-up session for the whole squad before splitting the players up into groups to work on various skills. The activities allowed everyone to become more used to the green, sandy surface, twisting, turning and running with the ball.

Pud was the only reluctant participant. 'I'm not built for all this sprinting,' he grunted, breathing heavily between goes at dribbling a ball through a slalom arrangement of cones. 'When are we gonna have a game?'

Jamie ignored him, showing wonderful balance as he glided through the obstacle course with well-practised ease. He passed the ball on to the next player and Ryan set off eagerly, but a little too quickly for his own good. He lost possession of the ball to the second cone he met and then tripped up over the fifth, sprawling full length.

'Red card!' bellowed Pud. 'Send that cone off – deliberate foul!'

Ryan was glad to be wearing a tracksuit – not just as protection against the cold, but against the coarse tufts of artificial grass. Mr Jones had warned them of the danger of burn grazes, if any bare arms, elbows and legs came heavily into contact with the astro-turf.

The boy grinned with embarrassment as he picked himself up and carried on rather more steadily. He was one of the players whose trainers didn't have moulded, patterned soles for extra grip, and the early evening frost was already making some areas of the pitch quite slippery.

They were all pleased when the chance came to pull on their coloured training bibs for a seven-a-side game, Reds versus Yellows. Chris, in the

Yellows' goal, knew he had the weaker side in front of him, but he didn't mind that. It was bound to give him more practice – and keep him warmer!

He didn't expect to let a goal in with the first shot he faced, though – and especially not from Philip, as the big defender, more noted for his heading than his shooting, let fly from long range. The ball kept lower than Chris anticipated, skimming under his body into the goal.

'One–nil!' shouted Jamie. 'Easy! Easy!'

Chris ruefully picked the ball out of the tangled netting and resumed play by rolling it out to Jordan, the school's right-back. Jordan played a neat one-two pass with a teammate to start up a move that was finished by Pud hoofing a shot over the low crossbar at the other end.

'Stupid little goal,' Pud fumed. 'Why don't we play with proper ones?'

Chris was right about being kept busy. The lively Reds' attack of Jamie and Ryan caused his defence all sorts of problems. Without Chris, it might have been a massacre, but even he couldn't prevent Jamie helping himself to a hat-trick and supplying a couple of goals for Ryan.

Chris wasn't at all happy with his footwear. He'd slipped several times going for shots and failed to lay a glove on the ball. 'Have to get a pair of those special trainers,' he sighed. 'These are no good on here.'

Andrew came over to lean casually on the goalposts. 'Been talking to Carl,' he began. 'He says Selworth School come to train on here a lot, too, and I suggested you could all have a tournament together.'

'What, with just three schools?' snorted Chris.

'Why not?' said Andrew. 'It's called a triangular tournament.'

At that moment they saw Carl and the Highgate teacher heading towards Mr Jones. 'Guess they must have fancied the idea, anyway,' laughed Andrew. 'Be better than just practising here on your own, I reckon.'

'Hmm, a floodlit football tournament.' Chris nodded. 'I'm beginning to like the sound of that myself!'

'Are these for me?' Chris gasped.

Grandad chuckled with pleasure at Chris's excitement as the boy tore off his school shoes to try on the brand-new trainers. 'How do they feel?'

'Fantastic!' Chris whooped. 'Just perfect. Proper astro-turf ones! Thanks, Grandad, you're amazing. I'd no idea you were buying me these. I've been pestering Mum about some.'

'I know.' Grandad smiled, glancing out of his kitchen window at the snow-covered recreation ground. 'Want to go and try them out on the recky?'

Chris shook his head as he stamped

around on the tiled floor. 'No! Snow's too deep. Don't want to get them all messed up out there. I'll save their debut till the Sevens tournament starts tomorrow night.'

'Might be best. Andrew can wear his then as well.'

'He's not even playing,' Chris laughed. 'Have you got him a pair too?'

'Of course. Can't treat one and not the other, can I?' Grandad said. 'Who are you up against first in the Sevens?'

'Selworth, and then Highgate,' Chris answered. 'It's a round-robin type tournament, you know, where every team meets each other in a group. Only we're all going to do it twice over, playing next week as well!'

Grandad nodded slowly. 'I see – I think.'

'And then we're going to have a final play-off between the top two.'

'Good idea,' agreed Grandad. 'Gives you another game, that's the main thing – more practice.'

'If we make it to the play-off,' Chris added doubtfully. 'Selworth and Highgate are both more used to that all-weather surface than we are. They've got to be favourites.'

'Favourites don't always win,' Grandad said wisely, nudging Chris on the arm with his elbow and slipping him a wink.

3 Round-Robin

The following night the home town team of Selworth kicked off the floodlit triangular tournament. Looking cool – and braving the cold – in their light-blue shirts and matching tracksuit bottoms, they passed the ball around cleverly and confidently on the smooth surface.

'Get stuck in, Danebridge!' yelled Andrew from the side of the pitch. 'They're toying with you, making you look like dummies.'

Andrew felt frustrated, unable to go and put in a few crunching tackles himself. He'd already charged about in the warm-up in his new trainers, using his extra height and weight unfairly against the younger lads. Much to his annoyance, though, he had failed to score past his kid brother.

But Selworth did. Chris was well beaten by a firm drive and was grateful to see another effort clip the post and go out for a goal-kick. He clapped his gloved hands together — not so much to keep himself warm, as Selworth were already making things hot enough for him, but to urge his team on. 'C'mon the Reds!' he cried. 'Mark tighter.'

The Danebridge players were wearing the school's red, numbered bibs over their own tracksuits, and

the number five scratched his head in bewilderment. 'How many men have they got on the pitch?' Philip asked. 'Can't keep track of them all.'

'Same as us, Phil, just the seven,' Chris assured him. 'I've already counted!'

Chris kept them in the game with two well-judged saves, but was left stranded when Selworth did increase the lead just before half-time. Their captain and leading scorer, Dinesh, totally unmarked, had an easy tap-in goal to finish off a pacy move that sliced open the Danebridge defence.

Mr Jones reorganized their formation, bringing on a sub and asking Jamie to play deeper in midfield. 'That'll mean you, David, being up front on your own, I'm afraid, but see what you can do.'

Pud shrugged and saved his grumbles until he stood with Jamie, waiting to kick off the second period. 'Huh! Can't do anything if I don't get given the ball. The only times I've touched it is when we've done this.'

'They're showing us how to play on here,' Jamie replied. 'Keep the ball on the deck and knock it about, that's the way. Their players move real quick

into space for each other.'

'You getting at me, Titch?'

Jamie grinned. 'Well, you're not exactly the fastest thing on two legs, are you, Big Fellow?'

'What about you?' Pud snapped as the whistle blew. '*You* never pass the ball. You just dribble yourself inside out till you lose it.'

Pud was perhaps the most surprised player on the pitch when Jamie went and passed the ball straight back to him. 'Go on, then,' he said. 'There you are, you have it. Now what are you going to do with it?'

Pud never had chance to decide. He was robbed instantly and he waved his fist at Jamie's smirking face. When the ball did come his way again later, Pud was more prepared and demonstrated his shooting powers by rattling the Selworth crossbar. It was

Danebridge's first worthwhile shot of the game and Ryan was alert enough to snap up the loose ball and bundle it into the net.

The goal failed to spark off any comeback. The football traffic remained one-way, bearing down on Chris's area like a city centre in the rush hour. It was something of a minor miracle that no further goals were conceded — thanks partly to

Chris, but also to some large slices of luck.

'Good job our goal difference didn't suffer too much,' the headmaster said. 'Only lost two—one. They might have run up double figures.'

'I could do with a bit of a breather,' wheezed Philip. 'How much rest have we got, Mr Jones, before our next game?'

'None! You're back on straightaway. Highgate will be fresh and raring to go, but we can't play as badly as that again, surely.'

'Big effort, team!' Chris cried out from his goal before the match began. 'We just froze against Selworth.'

'Not surprising in this weather,' Philip said, wearing gloves like most of the players. 'But now we might catch Carl's lot cold at the start. They've been kept hanging around, shivering, waiting to come on.'

Philip's hopes were misplaced. Highgate were too good a team to be caught napping, but at least this game was more of an even contest. Each side enjoyed its fair share of attacking, scoring a goal apiece by half-time, with Carl not yet able to break free of Philip's shackles.

'You've been sticking so close to Carl, I thought you might even go and stand next to him during their team talk,' joked Jamie at the break.

Philip grinned. 'Good goal of yours, Little'un. A real fizzer!'

Only Chris wasn't satisfied with his own performance. 'Sorry about their equalizer, gang,' he murmured, shaking his head sadly. 'Just lost the ball somehow in the floodlights. I'll bring a cap next week so I don't get dazzled by them again.'

Two hard matches in succession, however, began to take their toll of the Danebridge energies. Legs grew tired, allowing Carl Diamond more freedom to stamp his class on the game. The tall black striker, an imposing figure in his all-white outfit, controlled most of Highgate's moves and it was no surprise when he put them ahead.

Carl received the ball in space as he sauntered over the halfway line, looked around as if to pass, and then decided to go it alone – as usual.

'Close him down!' Chris screamed. 'Don't let him run at you.'

Too late. Carl accelerated frighteningly fast, bursting past Ryan and Jamie, with the back-pedalling Philip in no position to challenge as Carl let

rip in full stride. Chris did well even to get a hand to the swirling shot before the ball buried itself in the netting behind him.

'C'mon, they haven't won yet,' Chris shouted. 'Fight back, men.'

If there was going to be a chance to hit back, Chris knew this was it. Teams sometimes went and let a soft goal in themselves straight after scoring, and now Highgate paid the price of falling for the sucker punch. While they were still dreaming of glory, Jamie was allowed to jink his way past two half-hearted tackles and level the scores once more.

Carl was furious with his players. 'You're useless!' he roared. 'You just let that little kid walk right through you.'

The sulking Carl seemed to lose interest in the game after that, but

Philip was well aware of Carl's moods. He knew the threat of danger was still there, like a simmering volcano that could suddenly blow its top and erupt into action.

And explode Carl did, without warning, surging forward with the ball in the very last seconds. Philip managed to block the first shot with his long outstretched leg, but Carl pounced again and scooped the rebound up towards the top corner. Chris flung himself to the right, straining his body just far enough to fingertip the ball over the bar.

The 2–2 draw left Danebridge with only a single point to show for their efforts. They stood huddled in coats around the pitch to watch the night's final game, not knowing what kind of result would suit them best.

In the end, however, Selworth felt just as helpless. They were made to look a shadow of the side that had so outplayed Danebridge earlier. Carl was determined to take his frustrations out on somebody and he simply blew them apart. It was a one-man wonder-show of soccer skills, and his superb hat-trick in a 3–1 victory fired Highgate to the top of the group table after the first round of games.

	P	W	D	L	F	A	Pts
Highgate	2	1	1	0	5	3	4
Selworth	2	1	0	1	3	4	3
Danebridge	2	0	1	1	3	4	1

4 Go for Goals

'Bottom of the table!' moaned Pud. 'We've got no chance of qualifying for the Final now.'

'Course we have,' Chris insisted. 'We've still got two more matches to play next week. Anything can happen yet.'

'Oh, yeah, sure! Selworth are too good for us, and if that bighead Carl turns it on, we've had it.'

'Rubbish!' scoffed Philip. 'Football doesn't work like that. Every game's different. Just needs a bit of skill or luck or . . .'

'Or somebody not falling over when they should have scored!' Jamie chipped in, glancing sidelong in Pud's direction. He was ready to bolt across the snow-covered playground if Pud made a sudden grab for him.

'Can't help it if I slipped,' Pud said in disgust. They might even have beaten Highgate, if his left foot hadn't slid away as he prepared to hit a master-blaster with his right. 'My trainers have worn too smooth and we can't afford any new ones.'

It was a serious problem that Chris had already considered. They needed Pud's firepower up front, but he'd been almost like a passenger so far, unable to keep his feet when trying to turn on the artificial surface.

'What size do you take?' he asked.

'Sevens, why?'

'Sevens!' Jamie gasped. 'Mine are only twos. Pud must be a Bigfoot!'

They all laughed as Pud reddened, but Chris managed to smooth his ruffled feathers. 'It's OK, Pud, forget it. I think I know somebody who might just be able to help us out . . .'

The following week Andrew stood grumpily on the sidelines in his old trainers. It had cost Chris half his pocket money to bribe his brother to lend his new ones, but he considered the sacrifice worthwhile. At least, that is, if they helped Pud to move about properly.

'No sweat! I'll be all right now,' Pud beamed. 'And, anyway, even if I'm not, Jonesy's got nobody else to replace me!'

Danebridge had lost their substitute.

A phone message informed them that his dad's car had spun into a ditch on an icy country road. Nobody was hurt, but the car was out of action and the boy couldn't play.

Despite this setback, Danebridge's evening got off to a flying start and the captain's expensive gamble paid off sooner than he dared hope.

Jordan's long clearance found Pud deep in Selworth territory and it looked at first as if the striker was winding himself up to shoot. Feeling more confident with his better grip, however, Pud knocked the ball further on instead. He let the nearest challenger bounce off him and then crashed the ball goalwards. The keeper, Aaron, got both hands to the ball – and immediately regretted it. His pain was made worse by seeing the ball spinning around in the bottom of the net.

Selworth had expected to win comfortably again, but this time met with far more determined resistance. Defenders Philip, Jordan and Tom tackled like tanks, Ryan and Jamie worked hard in midfield and, behind them all, Chris was in top form. He stopped anything that escaped his teammates, making save after save, and it wasn't until late in the game that Selworth finally scored a deserved equalizer. A half-hit shot was turned wide of a wrong-footed Chris by the lurking Dinesh.

'Tough luck,' said Aaron as the two goalkeepers shook hands after the 1–1 draw. 'Thought we'd never get the ball past you tonight.'

Chris tried to rally his troops. 'Right, team, we've just shown how well we can play on here. If we can get three points by beating Highgate, we'll leap-frog above them and Selworth in the group.'

'They've got to play each other yet, remember,' Philip put in.

'OK, but they can't both win, can they? Every goal could be crucial. It might all come down to goal difference, if we're level on points.'

'So what are we waiting for?' cried Pud. 'Let's go for goals!'

That was much easier said than done. Danebridge failed to score at all in the first half and trailed 1–0 as they changed ends.

'You lot are history!' Carl Diamond taunted them. 'You might as well pack up your gear and go home. It's just between us and Selworth now.'

It did look that way. Chris knew that even a draw would be of no use. It was win or bust. 'C'mon, team,' he called out. 'If you want to play another match – and shut his big mouth – it's got to be all-out attack this half.'

Highgate's goal still rankled with Chris. He didn't like letting one in at the best of times, but the way Carl had scored made it even worse. The striker had slammed into little Jamie with bone-jarring force to win the ball, sending him sprawling backwards across the hard surface. The Danebridge players appealed in vain

for a foul. To their amazement, the referee waved play on, allowing Carl to elbow Tom aside as well before steering his shot under the diving Chris.

Jamie nursed a personal grudge, too, and wanted to exact revenge on Carl in the manner that he knew would hurt the most. Not physically, but mentally – by making him taste defeat.

First, however, Carl almost put the game beyond Danebridge's reach. He muscled his way past Philip and sent a left-footed curler towards goal. A cry of triumph had to be stifled in his throat as, for once, the keeper's ability matched his own. Chris managed to get his body right behind the line of the ball and clutched it safely to his chest.

Shortly afterwards, Danebridge levelled the scores — and then went in front themselves: two goals in a minute that killed Highgate off, a double blow from which they were unable to recover.

Though none of his own team would have dared to do it, fingers of blame deserved to be pointed at the Highgate captain for the equalizer. It was a sweet moment that Jamie relished, seizing his chance to catch Carl off guard. As Carl sidestepped a challenge from Jordan on the halfway line, Jamie sneaked up from behind to nip the ball off his toes.

Carl aimed a wild kick at Jamie but he was gone, whipping a pass out to Ryan on the wing and calling for the return. When it came, it was too far in front of Jamie but the ball ran into Pud's path instead and he walloped it home. The keeper had no chance to prevent the second either as Ryan was put through by Tom to net the decisive goal.

Carl's shrieks of complaint at his teammates were so embarrassing that Highgate's teacher subbed him. That was the last straw for Carl. He snatched up his bag and headed for the changing rooms and the teacher made no attempt to stop him.

Danebridge's 2–1 victory assured their place in the Final. 'We're one point clear of the other teams and with a better goal difference than Selworth,' Mr Jones explained. 'So even if this last match ends in a draw, we'll still qualify.'

Pud had a nasty thought. 'But what if Selworth win?'

'We'd still be better off than Highgate,' the headmaster smiled.

'Extra maths for you tomorrow, David, I think, to work out league tables!'

Selworth did win, handsomely, taking full advantage of the missing Carl. The previous week's hat-trick hero had disappeared, rumoured to have gone home early in a huff, unable to face up to the humiliation.

Without their self-appointed super-star, the dispirited Highgate team slumped to a heavy 4–0 defeat, leaving them bottom of the group. The scene was now set for a Selworth–Danebridge Final.

	P	W	D	L	F	A	Pts
Selworth	4	2	1	1	8	5	7
Danebridge	4	1	2	1	6	6	5
Highgate	4	1	1	2	6	9	4

5 Shot in the Dark

'How are the trainers, Pud?' Andrew asked in the short rest break before the Final.

'Wicked! Think I'll keep them.'

'No way! They're on loan for one night only. Just make sure you don't damage them. Do you have to kick the ball so hard?'

'Yes, he does,' Chris butted in. 'Captain's orders! I want to see him warming that Selworth keeper's hands again.'

'I can't get the same power in these as my soccer boots,' Pud admitted. 'Give me real grass to play on any day.'

'You might not have too long to wait, then,' Andrew said.

'What do you mean?' asked Chris eagerly, pulling on his goalie gloves.

'Grandad's been inside to warm up a bit and heard the latest weather forecast. They reckon the big freeze is over. We're in for a thaw!'

It certainly didn't feel like it at the moment for the players. 'Forget the cold,' Mr Jones told them. 'Go out and enjoy this last game. Whatever the result, let's see you play some good football.'

The boys took him at his word. They were very keen to win the tournament, but wanted to show off a few of their new skills too. They had not been slow to learn how to play on the flat, all-weather surface and now gave Selworth as good as they got. It rained goals.

The Danebridge defence was the first to leak. Dinesh found a hole through the middle and Chris's brave block failed to prevent the ball trickling over the line. Then Selworth were in need of a brolly! Jamie, Pud and Ryan poured forward in search of the equalizer, linking up smoothly to allow Ryan to lash a shot past Aaron from close range.

The same player scored their second goal too, edging Danebridge in front after a clever free-kick routine. As Jamie ran over the ball, Pud lumbered up behind and Aaron's trembling wall of bodies braced themselves for the expected blast. Instead, Pud merely tapped the ball to his left

to give Ryan a clear sight of goal. He made no mistake.

That was when Danebridge's luck ran out. Just before the half-time breather, Jordan twisted over on his ankle as he went to make a tackle and crumpled up into a heap. The ever-alert Dinesh darted into the vacant space, demanding the ball. He got it, looked up and took aim, but his shot was going wide of the target until it struck Tom.

It was a cruel moment of misfortune for the defender. Tom had sprinted across goal to cover and could not get out of the way in time. The ball hit him on the knee and whistled past Chris to level the scores again.

'Do you want to carry on, Jordan?' the headmaster asked.

The boy nodded. 'Got to. There's no sub.'

'Doesn't matter. We'll just have to be one player short.'

Jordan insisted he was all right, but as he hobbled back onto the pitch for the second half, it was clear that he would not be able to play a full part in the game. His teammates knew they were up against it now, but Chris remained optimistic that his weakened side might yet conjure up a victory. And they did have their chances. Pud blazed one over the bar, Jamie screwed a shot wide after a wonderful dribble and Ryan missed a golden opportunity to bag a hat-trick.

Selworth were wasteful, too, and even Dinesh was guilty of losing his cool in front of goal. He fooled Philip by nutmegging the gangly centre-back, slipping the ball through his legs, but seemed to panic when faced by Chris and hammered it straight at the grateful keeper.

A minute later the two captains confronted each other again in a one-against-one duel. Jordan's lack of mobility allowed Dinesh to snap up a loose ball and cut inside for goal. He was tempted to try and dribble round Chris this time, but was still confident enough to have another shot.

As Dinesh drew back his foot to strike the ball, the lights went out.

Chris was aware of something whizzing past his head and then heard the dreaded sound of the net rippling behind him. Lots of shouts and screams rang out at the same time as the whole sports arena had been suddenly plunged into darkness. Total confusion reigned.

'Is everybody OK?'

'Don't be frightened.'

'What's happened?'

'All the floodlights have failed.'

'Must be a power cut.'

'It's these freezing temperatures.'

As Chris grew accustomed to the gloom, he saw the ball lying in the net and Dinesh leading his teammates in a wild dance of celebration.

'Hey! Hang on a minute!' the Danebridge captain called out. 'I didn't even see it.'

Pud complained loudly to the Highgate teacher who was refereeing the Final. 'C'mon, ref, that ain't fair! You can't count that.'

'No need to act like Carl, lad,' the teacher grinned. 'Don't worry, it's no goal. And if the lights don't come back on soon, there will be no more football tonight either!'

Some of the Selworth party made

feeble protests about the goal being disallowed, but most people saw it was the only sensible decision. Even so, Danebridge were the ones who finished up feeling frustrated.

After waiting a quarter of an hour, the floodlights remained off and the match was abandoned as a draw. Selworth, though, were declared the tournament winners for topping the group.

'Never mind, lads, you did your-selves proud,' said the headmaster as the players collected their belongings from the chilly changing rooms. 'It's not the end of the world. There's still lots of soccer left to catch up on this season.'

'Do you know what match we've got first, Mr Jones?' Chris asked.

'Yes, I arranged it this evening in fact,' he chuckled. 'It's at home, once the pitch is fit. And you've been seeing quite a lot of your opponents recently . . .'

'Not Highgate, I hope,' muttered Jamie, thinking of Carl.

'Can't be,' said Chris. 'We've already played them in the league.'

As the penny dropped, the room was in uproar. 'It'll be great to get

230

Selworth back on our own muddy recky,' grinned Philip. 'But I bet *they* won't be looking forward to it!'

'Yeah,' agreed Ryan, 'I reckon we would have gone on to beat them, if it hadn't been for this stupid power cut.'

'Dead right, there,' grunted Pud, taking off the trainers. 'They know we've still got a score to settle with 'em.'

Andrew moved in before Pud forgot about something in the excitement. 'Mine, I think,' he said, easing his trainers out of Pud's grip.

6 The Real Thing

'I'd almost forgotten what grass looked like!'

'Incredible how green it is!'

'Bet it'll feel weird playing on it again after that artificial stuff.'

The footballers were gazing over their small playing field next to the school. Patches of grass were beginning to show through the melting mounds of slushy ice and snow as the winter sunshine got on with its work.

'Won't be long now before we can play some *real* football,' Philip said.

'Real football?' queried Chris. 'What do you think we've been playing under floodlights – tiddlywinks?'

'We all know what he means,' said Pud. 'Can hardly wait till these lumps of snow have gone and I get my trusty old shooting boots on again.'

'No need to wait, if you don't want to,' Jamie replied. 'We could just use you as a heavy roller to flatten out the recky pitch.'

Jamie darted away to a safer distance as Pud made a move towards him. 'Imagine Pud all covered in snow,' he chortled. 'He wouldn't be Bigfoot any longer – he'd be the Abominable Snowman!'

That did it. Pud gave chase across the playground and they disappeared round the corner of the building –

straight into the patrolling head-master. All three of them finished in a soggy heap on the mushy tarmac.

'Er, sorry, Mr Jones,' Jamie began hesitantly, trying to suppress any giggles as the headmaster struggled back onto his feet. 'Just . . . er . . .'

Pud finished the excuse for him. 'Just proving to Freckles here – I mean, Jamie – that I can be quicker off the mark than he thinks!'

Mr Jones grimaced at the dirt all down the side of his clothes. 'Well, let's see how quickly you can both go round to my office now – *walking*!'

A week later, on a bright Saturday morning in February, Danebridge School's league soccer season was due to kick off again on the recky.

Unfortunately the frost had returned suddenly overnight. The grass was white-over and the ground hard and crisp underfoot. Mr Jones had warned the players about the bad weather forecast and they came prepared. Chris wouldn't be the only one wearing tracksuit bottoms and gloves.

'Is the game still on?' Chris asked when he arrived. He was desperate to play, despite the fact that he was starting a cold.

Philip grinned. 'Jonesy's already inspected the pitch and said it's playable. Got your all-weather trainers?'

Chris nodded, wiping his nose. 'And my cap. The sun's really low and dazzly this morning. Worse than those floodlights!'

Mr Jones gathered everyone together. 'It'll be good experience for you today in these conditions,' he told them. 'I'm afraid the pitch is too hard to take a stud, though. You'd be falling over all the time in boots.'

'Only got my old trainers,' Pud muttered to Chris.

'Sorry, Pud,' he apologized. 'Couldn't borrow Andrew's again. He needed them himself for his own school match this morning.'

Pud shrugged. 'I'll be OK, don't bother. Just keep picking me up!'

Grandad spoke to Chris from his favourite spot, leaning against his back garden wall. 'The surface is pretty bumpy and rutted so watch the bounce! Hmm, you don't look too good, m'boy. How are you feeling?'

'OK, Grandad, thanks,' Chris replied, unable to hide a sniffle.

Grandad looked at him hard. 'Does your mother know about this cold?'

Chris shook his head. 'Just woke up with it this morning.'

'Aye, well, take care. May the best team win, as I always say.'

'As long as it's us, eh?' grinned Chris.

There was a lot of banter between the Danebridge and Selworth squads in the wooden changing hut. This league match was very important to them, in terms of both pride and points, and the players were keyed up for it.

Dinesh won the toss and decided to kick towards the River Dane. 'Just to give you the sun in your eyes first half!' he smirked at Chris.

The goalkeeper shrugged. 'Fine, no problem. I'll be able to get a sun tan while old Aaron's kept busy picking the ball out of his net.'

Ball control was difficult on the firm, frosty ground, but the two sides still tried to play the same kind of skilful, passing game as in the Sevens. Grandad smiled, pleased to see Danebridge showing better teamwork now after their weeks of practice indoors and under lights.

He was even more delighted when

their opening goal came from a typical piece of patient, stylish play along the left touchline. The move began with an accurate throw from Chris out to Tom in space, who then swapped passes with Ryan and Jamie until the little winger was sent clear with only a single defender barring his path.

Jamie sold the boy a classic dummy, leaving him on the seat of his pants just like the headmaster in the playground. He then took on Aaron as well, shimmying neatly round the keeper and sidefooting the ball home.

Danebridge's lead didn't last long. Selworth's own efforts were rewarded before half-time with an equally well-taken goal. Their nimble forwards skated over the bobbly surface as if

they were back on the astro-turf, and Dinesh tucked the ball inside Chris's far post with great glee.

'C'mon, we're not going to let them beat us on our home patch,' Pud growled at the break. 'Let's get stuck into them, I'm goal-starved.'

'Oh, no! Pud's getting hungry again,' Jamie joked. 'Watch out, Selworth, the Abominable *Slow*-man is coming to gobble you up!'

Even Pud had to laugh and team spirits were high as they forced several quick corners at the start of the second half. Jamie swung the right-wing ones into the penalty area with his left foot and Pud drilled them across from the other side. The sound of Pud ploughing through the frosty layers of crunchy, crackling leaves near the corner flag was even louder than the noises he made in the school hall at lunch with his packets of crisps.

The deserved goal came not from Philip's head, but from the unlikely source of Jordan's. The full-back, his ankle no longer sore, timed his run perfectly to glance one of Jamie's deadly inswingers past the groping goalkeeper. It was Jordan's first-ever goal for the school.

Danebridge strangely relaxed their grip on the game after this, though, and Selworth took control. It was the turn of Chris's goal to face a period of bombardment, but the visitors came up against an inspired keeper.

Chris always relished being in the thick of the action and he forgot all about his runny nose: he was enjoying himself too much. When he emerged with the ball again, plastered with dirt from another mad scramble, his goalmouth looked as if it had been trampled by a whole family of Yeti!

He kicked the ball away upfield to gain a bit of a breathing space, and it reached Pud, who was parked in the slippery centre-circle. The number nine turned with difficulty and nearly fell as he bumbled forwards, looking around for help. For once, it wasn't there. All the other Danebridge players had been back in defence, trying to prevent a second equalizer.

Pud found himself confronted by two defenders and a long run towards goal. He didn't fancy it, knowing he'd easily get caught. Glancing up, he saw that Aaron was positioned right out near the edge of the penalty area and felt tempted to have a go. The goalkeeper never imagined that

anybody would even think of shooting from such a range. He was wrong.

Pud steadied himself, set his sights and then whacked the ball hard and high. It came out of the sun's glare and sailed goalwards, bang on target, and the keeper knew he was beaten. Aaron made a half-hearted attempt to get back, but could only watch as the ball soared over his head and plopped down, one bounce, into the billowing net.

The scorer was the only person on the recky not to see the amazing goal. As he struck the ball, Pud's standing foot had skidded from underneath him and he finished up spread-eagled on his back, winded and staring up into the clear blue sky. He lay there with a silly grin across his chubby face, too heavy for anyone to lift up, but there was plenty of him for his

laughing teammates to hug once he'd regained his feet!

Five minutes later the match was all over and Danebridge's 3–1 win kept them at the top of the league table. Already the boys were starting to dream – and chant – about winning the championship and the changing hut was too noisy a place for Grandad. He retired to his cosy kitchen.

He was on his second cup of tea by the time his grandson finally appeared in the doorway. 'Champions!' Chris croaked.

'Aye, maybe, but there's a long way to go yet,' Grandad chuckled. 'Come and sit down and get warm. I'll pour you a hot drink.'

Chris suddenly whipped out his hankie. 'Aaahh-chooo!!'

'Bless you, m'boy!' said Grandad. 'Well, I don't know, the big freeze might nearly be over at last, but now we've got the big sneeze!'

THE END

ABOUT THE AUTHOR

Rob Childs was born and grew up in Derby. His childhood ambition was to become an England cricketer or footballer – preferably both! After university, however, he went into teaching and taught in primary and high schools in Leicestershire, where he now lives. Always interested in school sports, he coached school teams and clubs across a range of sports, and ran area representative teams in football, cricket and athletics.

Recognizing a need for sports fiction for young readers, he decided to have a go at writing such stories himself and now has more than fifty books to his name, including the popular *The Big Match* series, published by Young Corgi Books.

Rob has now left teaching in order to be able to write full-time. Married to Joy, also a writer, Rob has a 'lassie' dog called Laddie and is also a keen photographer.